THE
PACT
OF THE
FORGOTTEN

William Hanske

Editor: Amy Savoy

ISBN: 979-8-9937131-1-3

Published by Eclipse & Dawn Press

Table of Contents

1

The Birth of Silence

THE FIRST STONES of the valley town were laid before memory was written, when the world was still more shadow than shape. The settlers came from the north, families bound by hardship and superstition, guided by the whisper of fresh water in a land thought barren. When they found it, the ground was soft and dark, the air cold and steady as if drawn from the lungs of the earth. They dug deep, widening the fissure until a spring revealed itself, pure and endless. They called it the Blessing, and the town of Aeloren grew around it.

    For a generation, the spring was life. The soil drank it, the livestock grew fat, and children's laughter carried across the fog that rolled down from the hills. But those born in the valley spoke of dreams: voices murmuring beneath the flow, words shaped like prayers and commands all at once. The oldest called it the wind; the younger ones said it called their names. No one spoke of the unease that settled in their bones, the dread that came with silence when the water ceased to run for even a moment.

Then came the first dry moon.

The spring turned to darkness, thick and glistening, smelling of iron and rot. Crops failed, and animals were found drained and pale near the well's mouth. The villagers prayed, but no god answered. One night, a child vanished, then another, and in their place, the water ran again, clear and sweet as before.

From that night, the townsfolk understood what the earth demanded.

A generation passed under the bargain. Each time the water slowed, another was taken, offered to what they now called the Devourer beneath the stone. They built shrines around the well, carved figures in its edges, and whispered old rites when the air grew still. The priests of the valley claimed that the Devourer was not a demon, but a keeper; its hunger necessary to balance the world. The sound of the sacrifices was muffled by bells, heavy bronze things cast by trembling hands, rung to drown out the cries of those given to the deep.

It was said one bell, the largest and first, stood apart from the others. It was forged from the gold of their own adornments: rings, pendants, and heirlooms of love melted together into one warding tone. The sound was pure and mournful, carrying across the valley like a voice remembering its own death. For a time, it held the darkness at bay.

But in every story that survives long enough to be believed, there comes a break.

A family lived near the ridge: a mother, father, and daughter. They were known for their kindness and for the daughter's strange sight. She saw things before they happened: storms, births, deaths. Some feared her, others worshiped her. When the father was chosen to be given to the well, the girl cried out that it was wrong, that the Devourer had changed, that it no longer kept balance but consumed it. Her mother tried to quiet her, but she ran to the priests, begging them to listen. They did not. That night, the bell was rung again.

In the morning, the well was overflowing.

The girl vanished soon after. Some said she threw herself into the spring to reunite with her father; others whispered that the Devourer had marked her blood for defiance. No one noticed a small, dull bell was half buried in the muck next to the well. The mother wandered the town, hollow-eyed and wordless, until she disappeared into the fog.

Their home was found empty but for carvings along the walls--: circles, eyes, and symbols no one recognized. Years later, when travelers stumbled upon the ruins, they said the marks glowed faintly in the dark.

The tiny bell, with origins unknown, lay cracked and blackened, buried in the mud beside the well.

By the time the last villagers abandoned the valley, nothing living remained near the spring. The ground itself seemed to breathe. The air hung heavy with the memory of prayers that had gone unanswered for centuries. Yet the records of that time persisted, etched into tablets, whispered by passing merchants, and hidden in temples across the region. They spoke of the Blessed Well of Aeloran and its guardian beneath, the one who devoured so that life could continue.

Years folded into centuries, and the valley became myth. The forests grew thick, the river changed its course, and the town's bones decayed and twisted. Yet the well remained.

The great bell, now cracked severely and spreading like black veins across the surface, remained barely hanging in the tower. Its tone long gone but its weight undiminished. And though no one came to ring it, sometimes, when the wind cut through the valley just right, the air seemed to hum: a vibration, low and sorrowful, like the memory of a name whispered across time.

In that stillness, beneath roots and ruin, something stirred; something that remembered the warmth of human blood and the sound of the girl's defiance.

The echo of her name slipped into the dark once more. Three centuries had passed.

In the depths of the night, as the village lay shrouded in darkness, a lone figure emerged from the shadows. Draped in tattered robes, their face obscured by a hood, the figure moved with purpose through the deserted streets.

As they reached the heart of the village, the figure paused before the ancient well, their gaze fixed on the moonlit waters below. With a whispered incantation, they raised their hands to the sky, calling upon the powers of the earth and the heavens.

The air crackled with energy as the figure spoke the words of an ancient pact, a promise made in desperation centuries ago by those who sought to escape the horrors that lurked within the village's depths and the sorrows above it. And as the last syllable fell from their lips, the waters of the well began to churn and roil, a gateway to realms beyond, opening before them.

From the depths of the well emerged the spirits of the forgotten, their forms twisted and tormented by centuries of imprisonment. With hollow eyes and anguished cries, they surged forth, their ethereal forms pulsating with an otherworldly light.

The figure watched in silence as the spirits swirled around them, their voices blending into a cacophony of sorrow and rage. But amidst the chaos, a single voice rose above the rest, a voice filled with determination and resolve.

It was the voice of a young girl, her spirit bound to the village by a tragic fate. With tears in her eyes and fire in her heart, she spoke of a prophecy foretold, a prophecy of salvation and redemption for those who dared to defy the darkness that held them captive. Her eyes glowed, much like the old carvings that were etched into the walls of a house that once stood nearby. She was then drug back down into the darkness in the well, consuming any light that came near it.

Then a small dirty, damaged, and tarnished bell rose out of the ground next to the well. It moved up in line of sight with the cloaked figure. Just then, the figure understood what must be done and moved by the girl's words, the figure raised their hands once more, channeling their power into a beacon of hope that pierced the night sky. As the light spread across the village, banishing the shadows that had long cloaked its streets, the spirits cried out in triumph, their shackles broken at last. The tiny bell was now glowing, the crack mended and it looked like it was brand new. It was now shining brightly with power which slowly diminished and then faded into the darkness.

But even as the dawn broke on the horizon, casting its golden light upon the village below, the figure knew that their work was far from over. For the pact they had made carried with it a heavy burden, one that would test the limits of their strength and courage in the days to come.

And as the figure vanished into the darkness once more, their fate intertwined with that of the village and its restless spirits, they vowed to never rest until the curse that had plagued them for so long was finally lifted, and the echoes of the past silenced forever.

The ritual had opened the way. Now others would come, drawn by the light that had pierced the veil, carried to finish what had begun centuries ago.

2

The Haunting

THE VILLAGE OF AELORAN had been forgotten for three centuries. Deep in the forest, where sunlight struggled to penetrate the canopy, the ruins lay shrouded in legend. Locals spoke of it in whispers, the cursed valley, the hungry well, the place where the dead would not rest. Few dared to venture near.

But the four friends had been dreaming of it for weeks.

Emma had seen it first in her dreams, crumbling stone walls, a well that breathed, and a voice calling her name. When she told her sister Lila, Lila had dreamed it too. Then Marcus. Then Jared.

They told themselves it was coincidence. Shared anxiety about their upcoming hiking trip, perhaps. But when Jared found the old survey map in the university archives, marked with a village that shouldn't exist, they knew they had to see it.

They arrived on a foggy autumn evening, the forest thick with shadows that seemed to watch them.

As they stepped cautiously into the village square, the air grew thick with an oppressive silence. The only sound was the rustling of leaves in the breeze and the distant cry of a lone crow. Unease settled over the group like a shroud as they moved deeper into the heart of the village.

Among the ruins, they discovered an old well, its stone walls covered in moss and ivy. Intrigued, they gathered around its edge, peering into the darkness below. But as they leaned closer, a cold wind swept through the village, extinguishing their flashlights and plunging them into darkness.

Panic set in as they scrambled to find their way out, but the village seemed to shift and twist around them, leading them deeper into its labyrinthine streets. Whispers echoed through the shadows, faint at first but growing louder with each passing moment.

They stumbled upon a crumbling church, its doors hanging from their hinges.

The bell tower above leaned at an angle that defied physics, as if the building itself were trying to pull away from the ground. Inside, the air was thick with the scent of decay, and the walls were adorned with faded frescoes depicting scenes of suffering and despair. Emma recognized one of them from one of her visions: a girl with dark hair standing before a well while villagers knelt around her. The girl's eyes had been scratched out. In the center of the nave stood an altar, upon which lay a book bound in cracked leather.

Against their better judgment, they approached the altar and opened the book, its pages brittle with age. Words written in a language long forgotten danced across the yellowed parchment, their meaning lost to all but the spirits that haunted the village.

Suddenly, the ground began to shake, and the walls of the church trembled as if alive. Shadows coalesced into twisted forms, their eyes glowing with malevolent intent. The friends screamed in terror as they realized the truth: the village was alive, a living prison for the souls trapped within its walls.

With nowhere left to run, they huddled together, their only hope for salvation resting in the hands of the forgotten spirits who cried out for release. But as the darkness closed in around them, they knew that some secrets were better left buried in the shadows.

3

The Bell Tower

JARED, LILA, MARCUS, AND EMMA, huddled in the ruined church, still trembling from the whispers that had crawled along the walls. The book lay open on the altar, its brittle pages fluttering though there was no wind. None of them wanted to touch it again.

"What the hell was that?" Jared whispered, his voice hoarse.

"No," Lila said, her arms wrapped tightly around herself. "The real question is… why do I feel like it's watching us?"

Marcus swung his flashlight toward the rafters, and the beam caught something that made his stomach drop. High above, where the roof had collapsed inward, he could see into the bell tower itself. And there, suspended in the open framework, hung something that made his stomach drop. Not a bell. Not exactly. It was a mass of iron and bone, twisted together, swaying gently as though some invisible hand pushed it.

"That wasn't there when we walked in," Emma said, her voice cracking.

The four of them stood frozen, their breaths shallow. Then the sound came: a hollow gong that rattled the floorboards beneath their feet. The thing hanging in the tower shifted, and with the movement came a whisper, low and guttural, vibrating through the church's stone walls.

It wasn't one voice. It was many, speaking in unison.

"You opened the book…"

Emma staggered back. "It's talking to us."

Lila shook her head violently. "No. It's warning us."

The altar groaned, the cracked leather book snapping shut on its own. Dust lifted in swirls, forming shapes: faces, distorted and silent, their mouths stretched wide in voiceless screams. Jared clutched his chest, suddenly short of breath, as if the very air in the church had turned to ash.

Marcus grabbed his arm. "We need to leave. NOW!"

But the church doors were no longer doors. The wooden frames melted into black stone, sealing them inside. And with each toll of the iron-bone bell, the floor buckled and shifted, the old pews sliding aside to reveal gaping holes in the ground.

From those holes came hands, skeletal, charred, and clawing upward. The smell of burned flesh and damp earth filled the air as the hands reached, grasping at ankles, tearing at shoes.

Emma screamed as a skeletal hand latched onto her leg, cold as ice. Jared and Marcus pulled her free, stumbling toward the only remaining path: the narrow stairway that led up into the bell tower itself.

Behind them, the whispers grew louder.

"Climb... climb to us... and see..."

The four fled upward, the spiral stairs groaning beneath their weight. Shadows coiled along the walls like snakes, and the higher they climbed, the stronger the tolling became, until it was no longer sound, but a vibration deep in their skulls.

When they reached the top, the sight froze them where they stood.

The bell wasn't just iron and bone. It was made of bodies. Faces pressed against the metal, their mouths opening and closing, releasing that terrible chorus of whispers. And in the center, suspended like a heart in a ribcage, was the girl from the whispers, the one from the painting. Her eyes were wide and unblinking, and when her lips parted, her voice cut through the others.

"You freed us… but now you belong to the village."

The tower shook violently, the stairs collapsing behind them.

They were trapped.

4

The Girl in the Bell

THE TOWER SWAYED as if it were a ship at sea, every groan of its timbers a warning of collapse. The four friends pressed themselves against the warped wooden floor, the highest point of the bell tower. The railing had long since rotted away, leaving nothing between them and a deadly fall. Too afraid to move closer to the grotesque bell that loomed above them, they huddled together in the small space.

Emma's breath came in ragged gasps. "That's her," she whispered, it felt like remembering rather than seeing. "She's inside it."

Lila shook her head, eyes wide with horror. "Not just inside. She's part of it."

The girl's pale face was framed by metal and bone, her hair dripping like strands of cobwebs. Her mouth opened wider than it should have, splitting at the corners with a wet tearing sound until it was a wound. The whispering stopped. For the first time, there was silence.

Then, she spoke.

"You should not have read the words. You have loosened the chains."

Jared, trembling but defiant, took a step forward. "What do you want from us?"

The bell quivered as if in answer. The faces pressed into its surface began to stir, their eyes opening one by one. Dozens of eyes, hollow, black pits, stared at him. The girl's voice did not come from her lips this time, but from all of them at once.

"Blood."

The floor cracked beneath Marcus's feet. He barely managed to leap back before jagged wood split apart, revealing the endless black void below. From that abyss came a sound, wet, gurgling, like the drowning gasps of someone buried alive.

Emma screamed as a skeletal arm burst upward, clawing through the wood. Unlike the brittle remains they'd seen below, this hand was fresh; its flesh torn and dripping, fingernails broken from frantic digging. It latched onto her wrist, its grip impossibly strong.

Jared and Marcus pulled at her desperately, but the hand only dragged harder, inch by inch, toward the hole. Emma's screams turned shrill, almost inhuman.

"Don't let go! Don't let me—"

And then, without warning, the hand released her. Emma collapsed into Jared's arms, sobbing, staring at her wrist. The flesh was blistered, blackened where the hand had touched her, as though the very life had been burned out of her skin.

The girl in the bell smiled, her eyes fixed on Emma.

"You carry the mark now. One by one, you will feed us. And when the last of you is taken, the village will be free."

The bell tolled again. The sound split their ears, rattled their teeth. Blood ran from Marcus's nose; Lila dropped to her knees, clutching her skull.

Through the ringing, Jared heard something else, a faint chime, delicate, metallic. He turned his head. A smaller bell, no larger than his palm, hung in the far corner of the tower, its surface carved with strange runes. Unlike the monstrous bell of bodies, this one gleamed faintly, untouched by decay.

He staggered toward it, instincts screaming. As his hand brushed the surface, the whispers faltered. The larger bell convulsed, the faces shrieking. The girl's expression twisted into fury.

"Do not touch that!"

The small bell was warm, pulsing in his hand like a heartbeat. Jared looked back at the others, his voice shaking.

"I think… I think this is the only way to fight it."

The girl's mouth opened, and the tower itself screamed.

The walls split, wood splintering outward, the night sky rushing in. Below, the village writhed, the streets heaving like flesh, houses bending and twisting as though alive. The church spire cracked in two, stone tumbling into the void.

Emma staggered to the broken edge, looking down at the transformation. Through the pain in her marks, understanding came. "We woke it up," she whispered. "Opening the book... touching the bell... we woke the whole village up."

And above it all, the grotesque bell swung wildly, the girl's face distorting into a mask of rage.

"You are ours. You cannot leave. The pact binds you now."

Jared tightened his grip on the small bell. Its surface burned against his skin, but he held it high.

"Then maybe it's time to break the pact."

The bell began to ring.

5

The Ringing Path

THE SMALL BELL RANG with a sound that didn't belong to the world they knew. Not metal, not air, but something deeper, like bones cracking under water. The monstrous bell above shrieked, the faces pressed into it writhing in agony. The girl's pale features twisted, splitting into dozens of overlapping expressions, each one screaming.

The tower shook violently. Floorboards cracked open. The spiral stair collapsed behind them entirely, leaving only one way forward: out through the shattered wall, where jagged beams pointed into the void like broken teeth.

Marcus clutched Jared's arm. "We've got to move, NOW!"

They scrambled toward the gap, the tower groaning beneath their weight. Emma's injured wrist throbbed, veins blackening up her arm, but she pushed forward, gasping with every step. Lila stumbled, caught herself, then froze. Her eyes went wide.

"Down there, look!"

The ground below was no longer still. The village streets twisted like veins under skin, houses folding into each other, doors opening and closing without hands. Between the shifting streets, a path of pale stones stretched out, glowing faintly in the dark, like stepping stones across a river of flesh.

"The bell's showing us a way out," Jared said, raising the small artifact again. Each time it chimed, the glowing path pulsed brighter.

"Or it's showing us the way deeper," Lila spat, her voice trembling.

Another toll from the massive bell cut off the argument. The girl's voice thundered through the collapsing tower.

"You cannot run. The path is mine."

The tower gave one final lurch. The floor split, and the four of them were thrown into open air. The fall should have killed them. But as they plummeted, the pale light from Jared's bell blazed brighter, and the air itself seemed to thicken, slowing their descent.

They landed hard on the warped ground below. Pain shot through Jared's chest; Marcus coughed blood. Emma screamed as her wrist flared with searing pain. But the pale path glowed ahead, pulsing like a heartbeat in the earth.

Jared hauled Emma up, his own ribs screaming in protest. "We follow it. No matter what."

They stumbled forward, the ground around them shifting like muscle under skin. From the darkness between the stones, hands clawed upward, fresh this time, not skeletal. Their fingernails tore free as they dragged themselves out of the earth, one after another. Dozens.

Lila gagged. "They're not just spirits. They're people. Buried alive."

The first of the risen lurched forward. Its skin was waxy, its mouth sewn shut with black thread. It reached for Marcus, who swung a broken beam like a club, splintering its skull. But as it fell, two more crawled out to take its place.

The pale stones flickered, threatening to vanish. Jared shook the small bell desperately. Its chime spread like a ripple, burning the hands that touched the stones. For a moment, the path was clear.

"Run!"

They sprinted across the glowing path, their lungs burning, hearts pounding. The dead surged alongside them, hurling themselves into the gaps, breaking their own bones to reach.

Emma stumbled, her injured arm pulling her down. Lila grabbed her, yanking her back just as a hand clawed at her ankle. Jared rang the bell again, the sound cracking the night, splitting the hand in two before it could drag Emma into the dark.

The path ended at the edge of the village square, before the old well. The same well they had peered into when all this began.

Only now, it was wide open, gaping, filled with black water that bubbled and frothed. Something vast moved beneath the surface.

The girl's voice rose from the depths, cold and triumphant.

"You cannot leave. To escape, you must descend. The village keeps its own."

The pale stones flickered and went out behind them. The dead screamed, surging forward.

Jared gripped the small bell tighter, staring at the black water.

"Down," he whispered. "It wants us down."

Marcus spat blood, wild-eyed. "That's suicide."

Emma, shaking, lifted her blistered arm. The veins had reached her shoulder. "If we don't go, I'll be gone anyway."

The water churned, and something vast brushed against the surface, something with scales.

Behind them, the dead closed in.

They had only one choice left.

6

The Descent

THE DEAD CLOSED IN, their sewn mouths straining as muffled wails leaked from the stitches. The pale path had vanished. Only the well remained, a black maw, wide enough to swallow them whole.

Jared didn't think. He clutched the small bell, looked back at Emma's blackened marks spreading toward her heart, and made his choice.

He dove first.

The fall was endless. Cold water swallowed him, pressing against his chest like a vice. Darkness wrapped around him so completely it felt alive, tugging at his limbs.

He kicked upward, but the surface was gone. The water had no ceiling.

Then—chime.

The bell in his hand rang on its own, its sound vibrating through the water. Pale light rippled outward, pushing the dark aside just enough for him to see. And what he saw nearly stopped his heart.

Bodies. Thousands of them. Suspended in the water, floating in every direction, eyes open and watching. Their lips moved, whispering without sound. Threads of hair drifted like seaweed; limbs twitched as though struggling to swim. But none of them rose.

A splash echoed from above. Marcus slammed into the water beside him, thrashing wildly. Then Emma. Then Lila. In the bell's pale light, Jared could see them falling through the darkness like stones, eyes wide with terror. The four of them clutched each other, their bubbles of breath mingling, hearts pounding. Jared raised the bell, and its light created a small sphere of visibility around them, everything beyond it was absolute black.

But the water wasn't just water. It moved.

Something vast stirred in the depths. The current shifted, pulling them downward, faster and faster. Jared tried to fight it, but the pull was irresistible. The bell rang again, but this time the light did not repel. Instead, it revealed.

Below them, carved into the very stone of the well, was a spiraling staircase of bone. The steps were slick, glistening, and impossibly large, like a staircase meant for something not human.

They were dragged down until their feet struck solid surface. The water hung above them as if creating a ceiling in this cavernous room as though some invisible force was holding it in place. The bodies and dangers that were in the water could be seen vaguely, like looking through a dark veil.

The remaining light from the bell diminished and shapes turned to shadow and disappeared into the abyss. The dark water would drip down from the pool above them onto the ground. It was thick, resembling a mix of blood and oil.

They stood there, coughing and trying to gain traction on the slick stone. Jared collapsed to his hands and knees, vomiting water.

They stood at the bottom of the well, but it was no simple pit. It was a cavern, stretching outward in all directions. Pale phosphorescent fungi clung to the walls, glowing faintly. The air reeked of rot and old earth.

Emma staggered, clutching her blackened arm. "This... this isn't under the village. It's beneath it. Way beneath it."

Marcus pressed his hand against the slick wall. "This place wasn't built by people."

The bell chimed softly, unbidden. The fungi responded, pulsing with light, revealing a tunnel ahead. It twisted downward like a throat.

Jared swallowed hard. "It wants us to go deeper."

"No." Lila's voice was sharp, trembling. "We keep following where it leads, and it drags us further into its game. Don't you get it? The village... this place... it feeds on us."

A low rumble shook the cavern. From the black water behind them, something surfaced, huge, scaled, its ridges scraping stone. They didn't see its face, but they felt its breath. Hot, rancid, wet.

The choice was gone. They ran.

Their footsteps echoed through the bone stair, every chime of the small bell illuminating carvings etched into the walls. The images showed figures kneeling before the well, cutting their own flesh, offering blood into the water. In the final carving, the water rose up to swallow them whole.

Emma's voice cracked. "It wasn't a curse… it was a bargain. They fed it to protect themselves."

Behind them, the scaled thing moved through the cavern, scraping against the walls. It didn't chase quickly. It didn't need to. It knew they had nowhere else to go.

The tunnel narrowed ahead, forming an archway of bone. Beyond it, they glimpsed a vast chamber lit by a red glow, throbbing like a heartbeat. The sound of rushing liquid filled the air, thick and heavy.

Jared rang the bell again. The sound was thin now, weaker, as though the darkness was swallowing it.

The girl's voice rose all around them, echoing through stone and bone.

"Welcome, children. You've reached the heart."

They stumbled through the archway into a chamber where the well ended.

But the village continued.

7

The Cavern of Chaos

THE CHAMBER YAWNED WIDE, a hollow space so massive their footsteps dissolved into endless echoes. The glow came from the walls themselves, veins of red light pulsing beneath the stone, as if they'd stepped inside the chest cavity of something still alive.

Emma pressed her unmarked hand against the wall. The glow pulsed once, matching her racing heartbeat. Her marked wrist blazed in response, as if recognizing something. She ripped her hand away with a strangled cry. "It's... alive."

Marcus gritted his teeth. "Then we don't touch anything."

The sound of dripping water echoed faintly, but it wasn't steady. It sped up, slowed down, like something breathing. The air here was humid and metallic, every breath tasting of iron.

Jared raised the small bell. Its surface had dulled, no longer gleaming faintly but absorbing the red glow around them. When he shook it, the chime was weak, barely audible. Still, the sound rippled along the walls, peeling back shadows just enough to reveal movement.

Figures.

Not corpses, not spirits. Living people.

They crouched against the cavern walls, naked, their skin pallid and stretched tight over bone. Their eyes reflected the red glow, wide and unblinking. None of them spoke. They only stared.

Lila stumbled backward. "Oh my God... there are survivors."

Emma shook her head violently. "No. Not survivors."

As if in answer, one of the pale figures tilted its head and scuttled forward on all fours, impossibly fast. Jared barely raised the bell in time. Its chime cut through the chamber, and the figure shrieked, its limbs contorting before it retreated back into the shadows.

The others hissed, dozens of glowing eyes blinking into view.

"They're kept down here," Jared whispered, his voice raw. "The pact didn't kill everyone. It left some alive. Fed them... changed them."

Marcus brandished his broken beam of wood. "Then we keep moving before they decide to try again."

The chamber stretched onward into a narrowing corridor, its floor slick with the red glow that pooled like blood. The sound of the scaled creature echoed faintly behind them, scraping stone, herding them forward.

Every step was torture. Emma limped badly now; the curse from her wrist had moved down her side past her hip and ended just above her knee. She could barely support her own weight. Jared had to hold her up, one arm around her waist. The pale watchers followed at a distance, crawling along the walls and ceiling, their movements silent except for the wet sound of skin dragging stone. The glow grew brighter the deeper they went, until the corridor opened into another cavern.

Here, the ground was covered in bones. Human bones. Piled high, brittle and broken, forming hills that crunched beneath their feet. The air was choking, thick with the dust of decay.

Emma coughed, her blackened veins spreading across her collarbone. She sank to her knees, trembling. "I can't… I can't keep up."

Jared knelt beside her, trying to lift her. "You don't have to. We'll get you out. We'll—"

The bones shifted beneath them. Not from their weight. From below.

Hands erupted upward, skeletal this time, clawing through the heaps of remains. Entire torsos pulled free, skulls split open yet jaws gnashing. The bone-pit writhed, hundreds of dead rising all at once.

The pale figures shrieked and retreated into the walls, fleeing the chaos. Even they feared what rose from the bones.

Marcus swung his beam wildly, knocking skulls apart, but for every corpse he broke another rose from the pile. Lila screamed as hands grabbed her ankles, dragging her downward. Jared struck them with the bell. The chime cracked the air, and for a moment the bone swarm faltered.

But the bell's sound was weaker than ever, its glow fading.

Emma's voice rose above the chaos, trembling and thin. "It's not going to last. The bell's dying." She clutched her chest, gasping. "And so am I."

The bone-pit surged, dragging them deeper into its clutching mass. The glow of the walls pulsed faster, like a frantic heartbeat. And somewhere beneath the bones, something larger stirred.

8

The Bone Pit

THE CAVERN FLOOR HEAVED like a living thing as the dead rose from their grave of bones. Ribs snapped underfoot, femurs split, skulls cracked open as skeletal hands clawed their way upward. The sound was deafening, a storm of grinding bone and hollow screams.

"Keep moving!" Marcus roared, swinging his wooden beam like a madman. Skulls shattered, spines splintered, but the swarm pressed closer, dragging at his legs.

Emma could barely stand, her weight heavy against Jared's side as he half-carried her. Her blackened veins had reached her collarbone, creeping toward her throat, her skin clammy and pale. Every breath was a struggle. Jared tried to pull her along, but the bone-pit was swallowing them faster than they could fight.

Then—crack.

The pile beneath them split, collapsing inward like quicksand. Bones gave way, tumbling into a gaping hole below. Jared barely managed to grab Emma before they both slipped. Marcus fell to his knees, clawing for stability. Lila screamed as the ground crumbled under her.

"LILA!" Jared shouted.

Her eyes locked with his just as the pit gave way completely. She slipped backward into the collapse, her scream echoing into the void. Jared lunged, fingertips brushing her hand, but missed.

She was gone.

For a terrible moment, Jared stared at the darkness where she'd fallen, his hand still outstretched. Then Emma's weight pulled him back, and Marcus was shouting his name, and the bones were still rising.

The bones shifted again, sealing the hole with a sickening crunch. Lila's scream cut off. Silence filled the cavern except for the grinding of restless skulls.

Emma's voice was a broken whisper. "She... she can't be gone." Tears streaked her pale face. "Not Lila. Not—" But her words dissolved into gasping breaths, the curse tightening around her lungs.

Jared's chest burned, his hands trembling as he clutched the fading bell. "She might not be. Not dead. Just... taken." He didn't believe it, but the words left his lips anyway.

Marcus stared at the heap where she'd vanished, his face hard and pale. "Then we find her. One way or another."

The dead pressed closer, skeletal fingers scraping at their skin. Jared shook the bell. The chime rang, faint and brittle, but just strong enough to peel back the swarm. In the wake of its sound, the bones shifted again, not closing this time, but opening.

A passage revealed itself. A narrow tunnel beneath the pit, its entrance jagged and lined with broken femurs, glowing faintly red from deep below.

Marcus helped Jared lift Emma. "That's where they took her." he said, though his voice carried more hope than certainty. "The pit opened after she fell. This tunnel... it has to lead there."

They stumbled into the tunnel as the swarm surged shut behind them, sealing the passage with another avalanche of bones. The sound of the collapse echoed until all that was left was the hiss of the red glow pulsing through the walls.

The tunnel was damp, the stone slick with a sheen of dark slime. The air was warmer here, heavy with the stench of decay. The glow lit the walls in trembling pulses, like veins filled with fire.

Jared tightened his grip on the small bell. Its warmth was fading. He could feel its heartbeat slowing in his hand.

"Whatever is down here," Marcus muttered, his voice raw, "it's not done with us. And it sure as hell isn't done with her."

Behind them, far up in the bone chamber, something massive let out a low groan, part roar, part exhale. The sound rolled down the tunnel like a tide.

They pressed deeper into the passage, unsure if they were pursuing Lila or following her into a fate worse than death.

And for the first time, Jared realized the whispers had stopped.

That silence was worse.

9

The Veins of the Village

THE TUNNEL NARROWED until they had to move single file, their shoulders brushing walls that pulsed with faint red light. The glow wasn't constant. It throbbed, rising and falling like a heartbeat, and with each pulse the stone seemed to shift, tightening around them.

Emma wheezed, clutching her blackened arm. The veins had spread across her collarbone, creeping toward her face. Her skin was cold, clammy. Jared kept a hand on her back, steadying her.

"We'll stop soon," he whispered.

She shook her head. "If we stop, it catches us. You heard it. The thing in the bones."

Marcus walked ahead, his wooden beam gripped like a weapon. His knuckles were white. "Don't waste your breath. Just move."

The passage bent downward in a spiral, every step sinking them deeper. Jared raised the small bell once more. It chimed, but the sound was hollow now, like metal cracking under strain. The light it cast was pale and thin, barely enough to hold back the shadows slithering at the edge of vision.

Then they heard it.

Drip.

Drip.

Drip.

Not water. Thicker. Heavier.

They turned a corner and entered another cavern. This one was smaller, round, its ceiling low and slick. At its center was a pool, black liquid that bubbled as though boiling, though no heat came from it. The drip was blood, trickling from cracks in the ceiling, feeding the pool.

Emma collapsed, Jared barely catching her before she hit the ground. She pressed a hand to her head, her marked wrist blazing with sudden heat. "It's calling me.

The marks... they're burning. It wants me to go in.".

Marcus caught her, pulling her back. "Don't look at it."

But Jared couldn't help it. As he stared into the pool, his reflection shifted. Not his own face, but Lila's. Her eyes wide, her mouth moving silently, like she was trying to scream through the surface.

"Jared…"

He stumbled back, the bell slipping in his grip. It rang once when it struck the stone floor, the sound sharp enough to shatter the vision. His reflection was gone. Only black water remained.

Emma sobbed. "She's alive. She's in it."

Marcus dragged Jared away from the pool, his voice low and furious. "That's not her. That's bait. It wants us to think she's down here waiting to be saved. But you saw it. It's just showing us what we'll lose."

Jared picked up the bell, holding it close. "No. I saw her. She's real. And she's somewhere beneath us." He needed it to be true. If Lila was gone, truly gone, then Emma would be next, and then—

The ground rumbled. Cracks split the cavern floor. From the black pool, something shifted, pressing upward against the surface like a body trapped beneath ice. Fingers. A hand. Then another.

The liquid began to spill over the edges, flowing toward them like a tide.

"Run" Marcus barked.

They fled down the next tunnel as the sound of the pool gurgled behind them, the liquid slapping against stone in pursuit. The red glow grew brighter the deeper they went, illuminating carvings on the tunnel walls. Not crude ones like above. These were detailed.

Figures kneeling before the well. A bell raised above them. Chains wrapping their throats. And in the deepest carving, a village swallowed whole beneath writhing roots, every building sinking like a stone in water.

The village hadn't been cursed. It had been fed.

Emma stumbled, whispering through her teeth. "We're not supposed to escape. We're supposed to replace them."

The tunnel ended in another chamber. This one was larger, its ceiling vanishing into darkness. At the center stood a structure carved from bone and stone, an altar, but larger than any human could need. Upon it lay chains, fresh with dark stains.

Jared tightened his grip on the bell, its surface nearly cold now.

Marcus looked at him grimly. "This is where they brought her. If she's still alive…"

He trailed off.

They didn't notice at first, but the whispers had returned. Not all around them this time. Just ahead. Just beyond the altar.

A voice they knew…

Lila's

10
Lila in the Dark

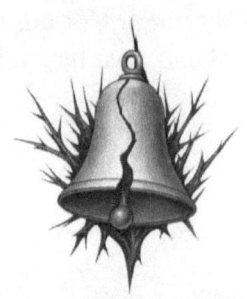

LILA OPENED HER EYES to silence. She was lying on stone, cold, damp, and faintly slick beneath her fingertips. The air smelled of copper and mildew. A faint red glow bled from cracks in the walls, pulsing like the beat of a massive heart.

She sat up slowly. No chains, no bindings. Just a wide chamber that stretched out into shadow, its edges lost in the pulsing red light. Her throat ached, raw, though she didn't remember screaming.

"Jared?" Her voice cracked against the cavern walls. No reply.

She pushed herself to her feet, every muscle stiff as though she'd been lying there for days. Had it been days? Hours? Minutes? Time felt strange here, stretched and compressed. Her boots scraped against the stone, and the sound echoed far too loudly.

Then she noticed the floor.

It wasn't stone. Not entirely.

Bones were embedded in it, fused into the rock itself, their twisted shapes smoothed down by time. Skulls jutted up like cobblestones. A femur here. A rib cage there. A floor made of the dead.

Lila's stomach turned.

The chamber pulsed again, the glow brightening, and in that light she saw something moving at the far end of the room.

A figure.

Tall. Thin. Its limbs too long, its body bent at odd angles, like joints had been placed wrong. It was watching her, but its face was obscured by the shadows. Not eyes, but hollows. Not a mouth, but a crack that spread wider the longer she looked.

It didn't move closer. It just stood, waiting.

Her legs screamed at her to run, but there was nowhere to go. Only the cavern stretching into deeper dark. And then she heard it.

The bell.

Faint. Fragile. Ringing from somewhere beyond the chamber. Jared's bell.

She clutched at the sound, heart racing. "Jared! I'm here!"

The figure twitched at her voice. Its head tilted, its body jerking like a broken marionette. The crack in its face widened, and from within poured a hiss, like steam escaping a kettle.

The bell rang again, closer this time.

And then whispers filled her head. Not around her. Inside. Dozens of voices overlapping, drowning out thought. They spoke her name, over and over, until it was no longer her own.

"Lila, Lila, Lila—"

She pressed her palms to her ears, screaming. "Stop!"

The whispers cut off.

When she opened her eyes, the figure was gone.

Only the red glow remained, pulsing stronger now, like whatever was at the heart of this place had begun to wake.

She staggered forward, chasing the fading echo of the bell. Each step carried her deeper, and yet she couldn't shake the sense that the cavern itself was guiding her. Closing behind her. Herding her forward.

Somewhere in the dark, Jared was calling her name. She clung to that. But underneath, she could still feel the whispers, coiled and waiting, like hooks in her mind.

What if the voice she heard wasn't his? What if it was just another way to pull her deeper?

And the thought that chilled her most wasn't that she had been lost.

It was that she had been found.

11
The Hollow Path

The glow dimmed as Lila pushed further into the passage, her fingers trailing along the damp wall to keep herself steady. The ground sloped downward, uneven, slick with some film that clung to her boots. The faint chime of the bell had vanished, swallowed by the cavern.

She slowed her breathing, forcing herself to listen. Nothing. Not even dripping water now. The silence was suffocating.

Her hand brushed against something smooth. Not stone. She jerked back. In the wall, half-sunken, was a face.

A human face. Eyes closed, mouth frozen in a silent cry. She stumbled backward, but more shapes emerged in the glow.

Dozens. Scores. The walls weren't stone at all. They were filled with people, bodies pressed into the surface like insects caught in amber. Some ancient, skeletal. Others disturbingly fresh, as though the stone had only just swallowed them.

Her pulse hammered. She wanted to run, but the passage narrowed again, forcing her forward.

The tunnel opened into a hollow chamber, its center occupied by something that should not have been there: a tree.

It rose from a fissure in the floor, its bark slick and black, its branches bare yet moving as if stirred by a wind she could not feel. Its roots burrowed into the bone-littered ground, pulsing faintly with that same red glow.

Lila approached, breath shaking. Something about it was wrong, not just its presence, but its sound. The tree wasn't silent. It breathed. And with each breath, the faces in the walls exhaled too, as if the tree was the lungs of this entire place, drawing them all in and out together.

As she circled it, she noticed the bark splitting, not with natural cracks but with carvings. Words. Names. Her own name. Carved over and over in hundreds of jagged hands.

Her throat tightened. She staggered back, her legs hitting something behind her. More bones, piled around the tree's base like offerings. The tree exhaled.

The breath carried whispers, curling around her like smoke. *Stay. Rest. Root.*

Her knees buckled. For a moment she almost gave in, sinking to the ground, her eyelids heavy. The pull was comforting, like lying down after days of exhaustion.

But then, faint and far away, she heard it again.

The bell.

It cut through the lull, sharp, desperate, breaking the spell. Her eyes snapped open.

The tree's roots had shifted. Slowly. They were no longer buried. They were reaching for her.

She bolted, stumbling down the nearest passage. Behind her, she heard the roots scraping stone, pulling the tree forward, or was it the tree pulling the roots? Either way, it was following. The whispers rose in fury, echoing in her skull. *Lila, don't leave. Lila, stay. Lila belongs.*

She ran until her lungs burned, until her legs gave out, collapsing against the cold stone. The whispers faded, replaced by silence. But she knew the tree hadn't stopped.

It had only let her go because it knew something she didn't.

Because she wasn't running away.

She was running toward.

Toward the heart.

12
Descending Evermore

THE TUNNEL NARROWED, walls pressing in so close Jared's shoulders scraped the stone. The red glow from the walls had dimmed here, leaving them in near darkness. Marcus had found an old lantern hanging from a rusted hook, its glass cracked but intact. He'd managed to coax a flame to life inside it, and now it cast wavering shadows across the stone, the light sputtering with every step.

"Careful," Marcus muttered, his hand braced against the wall. "If this goes out, we're blind."

Emma moved slowly behind him the best she could, dragging her leg. She held onto the back of his shirt as a guide, her hands uncontrollably shaking. She hadn't said much since they'd lost Lila. Every noise made her flinch. Jared kept glancing back at her, guilt knotting his chest. *I should've held onto her. Should've—*

The tunnel sloped downward until the stone beneath their feet changed. The floor grew uneven, crunching beneath their boots. At first Jared thought it was loose gravel. Then he noticed the shapes. Rounded. Hollow.

Skulls.

The lantern's light revealed more, scattered across the ground and pressed into the walls. Hundreds. Maybe thousands. The passage wasn't carved stone—. It was made of bone.

Emma gagged, hand over her mouth. Marcus swore under his breath.

Jared forced himself to keep moving. If he stopped, if he let the horror sink in too deep, he knew he'd freeze. He had to believe Lila was still alive somewhere ahead.

They pressed on until the tunnel split. Two paths. Both sloping deeper.

"Left or right?" Emma whispered.

Jared took the lantern from Marcus and crouched, sweeping the light across the floor. The left passage was coated in slime, glistening wet. The right was drier, but streaked with something dark. Drag marks.

And faintly, carved into the stone: **L.**

Just one letter, shallow, jagged, as though scratched with trembling hands.

"Lila," Jared whispered. His chest tightened.

Marcus frowned. "Could be a trap. Or bait. Whatever's down here wants us to follow."

Jared clenched his jaw. "Or it's her way of telling us she's still alive."

Emma moved closer, eyes fixed on the mark. "If she carved this… she's fighting to stay with us."

The silence pressed in, thicker than the air. From deep within the right-hand passage came a low sound, like breathing. Slow. Heavy. Not theirs.

Jared tightened his grip on the lantern. "We go right."

They stepped into the passage, each footfall echoing. The drag marks deepened, as if something had been pulled farther and farther along. Then the air grew colder. The walls closer. And the breathing louder.

Marcus stopped short. His face had gone pale. "Do you hear that?"

It wasn't just breathing anymore. It was whispering. Hundreds of voices overlapping, like a hive of murmurs spilling from the stone itself.

Emma whispered with pure terror, "it knows we're here."

The lantern flickered. Dimmed.

And ahead, etched into the wall with violent strokes, another mark appeared in the light: **ILA.**

The rest of her name.

Not finished.

Like she'd been dragged away before she could complete it.

13

Marks in the Dark

THEY PRESSED ON, one careful step at a time, the lantern's glow barely pushing back the black. The whispers never stopped. They rose and fell with no rhythm, sometimes low enough to mistake for wind, other times sharp enough to cut straight into the skull.

Emma flinched every time a voice hissed her name.

The drag marks thickened. Jared crouched once more, running his hand over the grooves. They weren't random. There were finger streaks beside them. She had clawed at the ground as something pulled her deeper.

"She's alive," he muttered, though his voice cracked. He needed to believe it.

Marcus scanned the walls, jaw tight. "Alive doesn't mean safe. Look at this."

The lantern revealed another mark, different this time. Not letters. Symbols. Circles crossed with jagged lines, repeating again and again. Some carved deep, some fresh enough the edges still glistened.

Emma leaned closer, whispering. "Those were on the well. Before we came down."

The air grew thicker, heavier, pressing down on their lungs. The passage widened just enough for the three of them to stand side by side, but the ceiling dipped low, forcing them to hunch.

Jared's shoulders brushed something hanging from above. He froze and lifted the lantern.

Bundles dangled from the stone, fabric, rope, sinew. At first he thought they were sacks of meat, until one shifted in the light and he saw hair. Human hair. Then an eye, half-open, staring at nothing. Then fingers, curled like claws.

Emma gasped, stumbling back. The bundles weren't sacks. They were people, cocooned in the stone, half-swallowed but not gone. Some shriveled. Some fresh. One twitched.

"Don't touch it," Marcus hissed, grabbing Jared's arm as he reached forward. "If they're alive, we can't help them without getting caught."

Jared's throat worked. He wanted to argue, but the truth was cold. He forced himself to turn away, though their muffled moans followed them.

The tunnel dipped again, then split into narrow cracks, each leading deeper. The drag marks veered left, but the whispers pressed from every direction now, so loud they almost drowned his thoughts.

Emma crouched suddenly, pointing. Another scratch in the stone. Not carved carefully this time, gouged in haste. **DON'T—**

The rest was cut off, swallowed by another drag.

They froze, the silence between them heavier than the whispers.

Jared whispered, "Don't what?"

No one answered. The lantern sputtered.

Somewhere ahead, deep in the black, something knocked. Three slow, deliberate strikes.

14

The Knock

THE SOUND CAME AGAIN, three slow knocks, echoing down the stone throat of the passage. Then silence.

Marcus raised a hand, signaling them to stop. Jared held the lantern high, the light wobbling with his trembling grip. Emma's breath rasped too loud in the hush.

The knocks turned into scraping. Something dragging itself along stone. Not fast. Not hurried. Patient.

"Back," Marcus hissed. "We need cover."

They pressed against the wall, hearts pounding. The passage was too tight to run, too close to hide. Jared felt the stone cold against his back and the sick certainty that whatever was coming knew exactly where they stood.

The lantern flame hissed again, dimming. Then it bloomed brighter, as if reacting to something near.

And in that glow, just for a heartbeat, the shape appeared.

Pale. Elongated. Wrong. A body stretched too thin, its limbs jointed where they shouldn't be. It crawled along the ceiling like a spider, head craning down toward them. Its face, or what should've been a face, was nothing but hollows, a suggestion of eyes, and a mouth that twitched open too wide.

Emma muffled a scream. Jared clamped a hand over her mouth.

The creature froze. It hung there, listening. Its head jerked toward them with an insect's twitch.

Then the whispers in the stone stopped. Every voice. All at once.

The silence was worse.

Marcus raised what was left of the broken board he had been using to defend the group… His voice was low, steady: "Go. Now."

But the moment Jared shifted his weight, the lantern flame flared, betraying their movement. The thing shrieked, high and thin, a sound that pierced bone, and launched.

Chaos. Jared pulled Emma toward the narrower crack to the left. She stumbled, Jared caught her and they sprinted. The lantern swung wild in Jared's hands, casting broken images of the thing's limbs as it crashed against the walls, stone shattering under its weight.

Marcus stayed behind, swinging wildly with what was left of the board. Jared caught a glimpse of his jagged makeshift weapon striking flesh, if it was flesh. Black fluid hissed onto the stone like acid, smoking where it touched.

"Run!" Marcus bellowed.

But the thing slammed Marcus against the wall with an inhuman crack. His board flung against the stone and finally shattered for good.

He didn't scream, only a choked grunt, then the creature dragged him upward, vanishing into the dark above.

Emma screamed his name. Jared grabbed her, hauling her down the passage as debris rained behind them. The whispers returned, swelling with laughter this time.

They ran until their lungs burned, until the sounds faded. They collapsed in a narrow alcove, gasping, the lantern guttering low.

Emma's hands shook violently, blood smeared across her arm, Marcus's blood, not hers. "He's alive," she whispered, voice breaking. "He has to be. Didn't you hear? He didn't, he didn't scream."

Jared pressed the heel of his palm against his forehead, trying to steady the nausea threatening to overtake him. He wanted to believe her. He wanted to cling to any hope.

But the image burned into his mind: Marcus vanishing upward into black, the creature's hollows staring down at him.

Alive. Or already gone.

There was no way to know.

And now there were only two.

15

The Bait of Hope

THEY DIDN'T STOP MOVING. To stop meant to think, and to think meant to picture Marcus vanishing into the ceiling. So Jared pushed Emma onward, one hand gripping hers, the other clutching the lantern as if it were the last real thing in the world.

The tunnel sloped downward, the air wet and heavy. The stone walls glistened as though they breathed. The whispers pressed harder, not in the same mocking chorus as before. These were fractured, hushed, like voices just beyond a door. Listening. Waiting.

Emma's voice broke the silence. "He's not dead. You saw him fight. Marcus, he's—"

Jared cut her off, harsher than he meant: "Quiet."

Her lips pressed tight, but her eyes shone with fury. She pulled her hand free, walking faster into the dark, as if anger could keep her from collapsing.

The tunnel forked again, three ways this time. Scratches marked the walls, not carved symbols this time, but desperate gouges, frantic lines clawed into the stone. Jared lifted the lantern. One line stood out among the chaos. Letters, jagged but legible.

LILA.

Emma gasped, her face brightening even in the dim glow. "She's alive. She's, she left this for us."

Before Jared could speak, something shifted down the left-most tunnel. A scrape, a soft thump, like something dragging its limbs. The lantern light didn't reach far enough, but Jared swore the darkness there felt thicker, watching.

Emma pointed to the middle path. "The name's this way. We follow her."

Jared hesitated, every instinct screaming at him to turn back, to hide, to do anything but keep pressing into the gut of this place. But then the lantern caught another faint mark: a thread of fabric snagged on the stone. Torn cloth, pale, like the sleeve of a dress.

Emma reached for it with trembling fingers. "It's hers."

They moved faster now, the whispers rising as if aware of their choice. The passage narrowed again, forcing them to turn sideways, their shoulders scraping damp walls. The lantern guttered, flame shrinking low, threatening to die.

Jared's stomach clenched. "Don't go out. Don't you dare go out—"

The flame pulsed once, then swelled brighter. Not from oil. From something else.

Ahead, down the black corridor, came the faintest sound. A human voice. Weak, almost lost beneath the whispers.

"...help..."

Emma froze, tears springing to her eyes. "That's her. Jared, that's Lila!"

The word echoed, swallowed by stone. Then silence.

And then, faintly, the sound of something else answering in the dark.

Not Lila.

Not human.

16
The Divide

THE SOUND CAME AGAIN, faint but real.

"...please... help..."

Emma pushed forward recklessly, scraping her shoulder against the stone as the passage opened into a wider chamber. Jared followed, lantern thrust high.

The light spilled out, casting jagged shadows across a cavern carved by water and time. The ceiling rose high above them, lost in blackness, and the ground sloped toward a deep fissure splitting the chamber in two. A chasm, narrow but impossibly deep, its bottom swallowed by echoes.

On the far side, curled against the wall, dress torn, hair matted with grime, was Lila.

Emma cried out, stumbling to the edge. "Lila! It's us!"

Lila's head jerked up. Her face was pale, hollow-eyed, but alive. Alive. She blinked against the lantern light, lifting a trembling hand. "Emma?"

The sound of her voice cracked Jared's chest open. After everything, she was still here.

But between them lay the divide.

Emma dropped to her knees, reaching across the gap, fingers clawing the air uselessly. "We found you! Hold on, we'll get to you!"

Lila shook her head, her lips trembling. "You can't. It won't let you."

Jared felt the whispers coil tighter around his skull, louder here, as if the fissure itself fed them. He leaned out, scanning for a way across. The stone edges crumbled under his boots. A jump was suicide. No bridge, no handholds. Only emptiness yawning below.

"Lila, listen to me," Jared said, forcing his voice steady. "Stay awake. Don't move. We'll find another way to you."

Lila's eyes darted toward the darkness above her, then back at them. "It's not just the dark. It's in the walls. It listens."

Emma sobbed. "We're so close. We can't just leave you—"

The air shifted. From the far tunnel behind Lila, a shape moved. Slow, deliberate.

Jared's stomach dropped.

"Emma, back away."

But Emma wouldn't. She stayed at the edge, hand outstretched, her voice breaking: "Run, Lila! Please, run!"

Lila tried to stand, staggering against the wall, her body weak. Her eyes locked on Jared's. For a heartbeat, there was something unspoken there, desperation, but also warning.

Then the whispers surged, drowning all thought.

The thing in the tunnel behind her stepped closer.

17

Pulled Below

"RUN!" EMMA SCREAMED. Lila stumbled toward the fissure's edge, but her legs buckled. She fell hard, palms scraping the stone. Behind her, the thing lurked closer, a hulking silhouette, its body wrong in ways the lantern couldn't fully reveal. Its arms scraped the walls, bending in ways no bones should.

Jared dropped to his stomach at the edge of the chasm, thrusting the lantern out to buy seconds of light. "Lila! Crawl to me!"

Her wide eyes locked on his. She dragged herself forward, nails tearing against the rock as she inched closer. The gap was too wide, but still she tried. Emma stretched out beside him, tears streaming, fingertips straining toward her sister.

For one glorious second, their hands almost touched.

Then the floor beneath Lila shuddered. From the fissure walls, slick black tendrils shot upward, lashing around her arms and waist.

She shrieked, jerking back, her hand slipping past Emma's.

"NO!" Emma lunged forward, nearly pitching herself into the pit. Jared yanked her back just in time, his grip iron around her shoulders. The stone crumbled where her knees had been.

The tendrils dragged Lila screaming into the darkness, pulling her down the far tunnel. Her voice echoed, ragged and raw, until it cut off, swallowed by the endless black.

Emma collapsed, sobbing into her hands. Jared knelt beside her, chest heaving, rage boiling beneath the helplessness. They had her. They almost had her.

The silence that followed was worse than the screams.

Until a sound rose from the far tunnel.

Footsteps.

Jared's breath caught as a figure emerged from the dark. For an instant, he thought the shadows mocked him. But no, there he was.

Marcus.

He limped forward, eyes hollow, his skin pale and damp with sweat. His shirt was torn, his arms streaked with dark stains. But something was wrong. His movements were too stiff, too careful, as if his body didn't quite remember how to work. And his eyes, though they looked at them, seemed to be focused on something far beyond.

Emma gasped, leaping to her feet. "Marcus! You're—" She stopped short, her words faltering.

Something was wrong.

His movements were sluggish, his face slack. When his eyes met theirs, Jared's stomach turned. They weren't vacant, but they weren't fully his either. The pupils were too wide, swallowing the color, and beneath his skin, faint dark lines traced his veins like spider webs.

Marcus swayed, lips parting. His voice was hoarse, raw. "It… let me go."

The whispers surged again, wrapping the chamber in a suffocating hum.

Jared tightened his grip on the lantern. Whatever had released Marcus hadn't done it for mercy.

18
Fracture Return

EMMA THREW HER ARMS around Marcus the moment he staggered close enough. He didn't resist, but his body felt stiff, like he wasn't sure how to respond. His arms lifted slowly, awkwardly, and then fell back to his sides.

Jared kept the lantern high, studying him. The light caught Marcus's face, and his gut twisted. The man's pupils were blown wide, swallowing nearly all the color. And beneath the grime, faint black veins shown across his neck and temples, pulsing as if alive.

Emma pulled back, her hands gripping his shoulders. "We thought you were dead."

Marcus gave her a small, strange smile. "Not dead. Not yet." His voice rasped like dry stone grinding together.

Jared frowned. "How'd you get out? We saw you fall."

Marcus swayed slightly, gaze drifting toward the fissure where Lila had been dragged away. "It caught me. The dark... it doesn't kill unless it wants to. It showed me... things. Promises. Then it let me go."

The words hung heavy in the chamber. Jared didn't like the way he said *let me go*.

Emma shook her head fiercely, though the movement made her wince, the black marks on her wrist and ankle throbbing. "I don't care. You're here, and that means we can fight together. We're going to save Lila and end this."

Marcus's smile lingered. Too long. "Yes. End it."

Jared stepped between them. "We keep moving. Lila's ahead of us somewhere, and whatever that thing is, it won't stop." He turned to Marcus. "You can walk?"

Marcus nodded once. "I can walk."

As they pressed deeper into the tunnel, Jared stayed half a step behind him. Marcus's stride was steady, but every so often his head tilted as though listening to something no one else could hear. And once, when Emma asked if he remembered the way out, his lips curled into a thin, knowing grin.

"We're already exactly where it wants us to be."

Jared gripped the lantern tighter, pulse hammering. Marcus was back. But he wasn't the same.

And Jared had no idea if he could still be trusted.

19

Shadows Between Them

THE TUNNEL NARROWED until Jared had to duck. His lantern guttered low, oil running thin, shadows licking the walls like hungry tongues. Every step echoed like a drumbeat in his skull.

Emma clung close, one hand on Marcus's arm as though afraid he might vanish again. Jared kept the rear, eyes never leaving Marcus's back.

"We need to find water," Jared muttered. His throat was raw from the stale air. "If we don't, we won't make it much longer down here."

Marcus didn't slow. "There's a stream ahead. Just beyond the split."

Jared's gut tightened. He hadn't seen the split yet. Neither had Emma. "And how would you know that?"

Marcus tilted his head, almost as if the question puzzled him. "I just... do."

Emma shot Jared a look. Defensive. "He's been down here longer than we have. Maybe he saw it."

But Jared had been watching Marcus since the moment they found him. His pace never wavered, like he was following a map etched into his mind. Or whispered in his ear.

Minutes later, the tunnel forked into two mouths yawning in opposite directions. Jared's skin prickled.

Marcus lifted a finger to the left path. "There."

And when they rounded the bend, the faint trickle of water greeted them. A narrow stream bled from the stone, running black but clear enough to cup in their hands.

Emma exhaled with a broken laugh, tears slipping down her face. "You saved us."

Jared crouched, filled his palm, and drank. It was bitter, metallic, but water all the same. Still, the unease in his chest only deepened. Marcus had known. Somehow.

As they rested, Jared noticed Marcus sitting apart, eyes closed, lips moving silently. Like he was listening. Or repeating.

"What are you doing?" Jared asked sharply.

Marcus's eyes opened slowly. Too slowly. "Praying."

Emma frowned. "You've never prayed before."

Marcus smiled faintly. "There's a first time for everything."

The lantern hissed as the flame shivered. Jared fed it the last of the oil, watching Marcus's reflection bend and twist in the wavering glass. The caves were eating at all of them. But Marcus? Marcus was changing. And Jared couldn't shake the thought that maybe, just maybe, the caves hadn't let him go at all.

20
The Drop

THE TUNNEL SLOPED DOWNWARD, slick with moisture. Jared's light revealed patches of moss glistening on the stone, making the footing treacherous.

"Careful," he warned, planting each step.

Emma followed, clutching the wall. Marcus brought up the rear this time, his silence pressing against Jared's back like a weight.

Halfway down the slope, Jared spotted it, a jagged crack in the stone yawning across the floor. A fissure, narrow but deep.

"We'll need to cross one at a time," Jared said. He tested the stone lip with his boot. It held.

He passed the lantern to Emma, then crouched and sprang. His boots scraped, barely catching the other side. His stomach lurched at the faint clatter of rocks tumbling into the darkness below.

"Okay," he called softly. "Emma, you're next."

She hesitated, eyes wide in the dim glow. Jared stretched out his arms. "You can make it. I've got you."

She leapt. Her fingers clutched his, and he hauled her across. Her sob of relief brushed his shoulder.

Now Marcus stood alone on the far side. The lantern-light caught the fissure between them, an uneven mouth ready to swallow him.

"Your turn," Jared said.

Marcus bent, coiling his legs. For an instant, Jared thought he saw Marcus's lips move again, silent, like before. Then he jumped.

The landing was too short. His foot slammed the edge, stone crumbling beneath it.

Emma screamed. Jared lunged, grabbing his wrist. His arm strained, tendons burning as Marcus's body dangled over the abyss.

"Hold on!" Jared roared.

Marcus's eyes locked with his, black pupils huge, face eerily calm. "Let me go."

"What?!" Jared's grip slipped.

"Let me go," Marcus repeated, voice low, too steady for someone hanging over a drop.

"No!" Emma shrieked. She scrambled to Jared's side, clutching his arm. Together, they dragged Marcus onto the ledge. He sprawled in the dirt, chest heaving.

Emma clutched him, sobbing. "You nearly died. Don't you ever, don't you ever say that again!"

Marcus only smiled, eyes drifting toward the dark. "Death isn't what you think it is. Not down here."

Jared's stomach twisted. The crack in the stone wasn't the only fissure forming. Something was fracturing between them, invisible but deepening with every step.

21

The Lantern's Hunger

BY THE TIME THEY STOPPED to rest again, the lantern's flame was little more than a quivering bead of light. The air tasted of damp stone and rust, and the silence pressed so heavily that Emma had to whisper just to hear her own voice.

"We're almost out of oil," Jared said, shaking the lantern gently. The faint slosh at the bottom made his stomach sink. "Maybe an hour. Two at most."

Emma buried her face in her hands. "If the light goes out down here…"

She didn't finish. She didn't need to. The dark was alive. They all felt it.

Jared turned to Marcus, who sat with his back to the wall, eyes distant. "Unless you've got a miracle tucked away, we're done."

Marcus blinked slowly, and then stood without a word. He walked to the edge of the tunnel, running his fingers along the wall as if reading invisible script. Then he pushed aside a cluster of loose rock. Beneath, half-buried in dirt, was a small clay vessel.

Jared's heart hammered. "What the hell…"

Marcus knelt, brushing dust away. The vessel sloshed faintly when he lifted it. He pulled the stopper, and the sharp, oily scent made Jared's eyes water.

Lantern fuel.

Emma gasped. "Oh my god. How did you…?"

Marcus tilted his head, as if confused by the question. "I knew it was here."

Jared stared at him, throat dry. "Knew? How could you possibly—"

"Because it wanted me to," Marcus said softly, almost reverently. He poured the liquid into the lantern, and the flame leapt back to life, brighter, steadier. Shadows retreated, but Jared's unease only grew.

Emma clutched Marcus's arm, relief breaking across her face. "You saved us again."

Jared saw it differently. His gut whispered what Emma refused to hear: the caves didn't leave gifts lying around. If Marcus had found fuel, it was because the thing in the dark wanted them to have it.

And if it wanted them alive… the question was why.

22

Whispers in the Stone

THE TUNNELS TIGHTENED as they moved, the ceiling dipping so low they had to crawl. Their knees scraped raw against the stone, and the air grew heavy with mildew and rot.

Emma's breath rasped behind Jared, ragged with exhaustion. "We... can't keep this up much longer."

"We don't have a choice," Jared muttered. His shoulders ached, the lantern bumping with every movement. The memory of its dimming flame gnawed at him, even though Marcus's "miracle" had bought them more time.

Ahead, the tunnel split once more. One path sloped upward, jagged and narrow. The other dropped into a throat of darkness.

Jared paused. "Which way?"

Emma leaned against the wall, trembling. "Up. Please. If it's a way out—"

But Marcus moved past them, crouching at the mouth of the downward path. He pressed his ear to the stone, eyes half-closed. For a long, unsettling moment, he didn't move.

"Down," he said finally. "The air is fresher that way."

Emma blinked at him. "How do you know that?"

Marcus didn't answer. He simply adjusted the straps on his pack and started forward.

Jared's jaw tightened. "Hold on." He crouched by the wall Marcus had touched. Cold, lifeless rock. No draft. No sound but their own breathing. "There's nothing here. You can't hear anything."

Marcus turned his head, expression unreadable in the lantern glow. "You don't listen hard enough."

The words chilled Jared worse than the stone beneath his hand.

Emma hesitated, looking between them. Then, with a shaky breath, she followed Marcus. "He hasn't been wrong yet," she whispered.

Jared remained kneeling, staring into the split paths. The upward route tugged at him like instinct, but Emma was already gone, her shadow shrinking into the dark where Marcus led.

With a curse under his breath, Jared followed.

The downward tunnel swallowed them whole.

And though the air did feel cooler as they moved, Jared could not shake the sense that it wasn't a draft at all, but a breath.

Something was waiting.

23
The Fracture

THE TUNNEL WIDENED suddenly into a chamber where the ceiling soared high above them, its stone teeth glistening with moisture. Their lantern threw weak halos against the walls, unable to touch the black dome overhead.

Emma sank to the ground, gasping, "Just a minute. Please."

Jared set the lantern down, pacing the edges of the cavern. He ran his hand over the stone, cold, slick, unbroken. No markings, no sign of a way out. Just another trap.

Marcus stood in the center, still as a shadow. His eyes swept the ceiling, the walls, as though searching for something unseen.

Finally, Jared couldn't hold it in. "Alright. Enough."

Emma blinked at him. "What?"

He jabbed a finger toward Marcus. "He's not guessing. He's leading us somewhere. Down. Always down. And every time, it's like he already knows what we'll find."

Marcus's gaze slid to him, calm and unreadable. "Would you rather I let you wander blind? You'd already be dead without me."

"That's not the point," Jared snapped. His voice echoed off the stone. "The caves want us alive. You said it yourself: 'death isn't what we think it is down here.'" He stepped closer, eyes narrowing. "Whose side are you on, Marcus?"

Emma shot to her feet. "Jared, stop it! He saved us, twice! The fuel, the passages—"

"Exactly!" Jared cut her off. His hand trembled with the words. "Too convenient. Too perfect. Don't you get it? He's not saving us. He's keeping us alive long enough for whatever's down here to finish what it started."

Emma's eyes filled with tears, her voice breaking. "You don't mean that. You can't—"

But Marcus only watched them both, face unreadable, as though weighing something they couldn't see. His silence was worse than any denial.

Jared stepped back, lantern light quivering against the cavern walls. "Very soon I feel" he said, his voice hardening, "we're going to find out which side you're on. And I don't think we're going to like the answer."

The flame flickered, shadows closing in. None of them spoke again, but the chamber seemed smaller now, the silence sharper.

The fracture had begun.

24

The Pull

LILA WOKE to the sound of dripping water. Slow, steady, each drop echoing through the hollow chamber.

Her wrists throbbed where the rough stone had scraped her raw, though no chains bound her. The cave itself was her prison, the walls curving inward like ribs, the floor uneven and slick with slime.

The dark pressed close, heavier than before. Yet she could see. Not clearly, not like lantern-light, but with a faint, sickly glow that seemed to seep from the stone itself. Shadows bent the wrong way, light curling where no flame burned.

She pushed herself up, every muscle aching. "Hello?" Her voice wavered, swallowed almost instantly by the cavern. "Is anyone there?"

Something answered. Not with words, but with a tremor beneath her feet, a pulse that traveled through the rock. For a fleeting moment, she thought she felt it in her chest, like a second heartbeat.

Her breath caught. She stumbled forward, hands sliding over the wall. The stone felt warm. Alive.

And then, voices. Distant, muffled, carried by the stone like whispers underwater. Familiar. Jared. Emma.

Her throat tightened. "I'm here!" she screamed, pounding her fists against the wall. "I'm right here!"

The whispers cut off. Silence rushed back in.

Before she could call again, the floor beneath her lurched. A fissure split open, narrow but deep, and a gust of air pulled at her hair and clothes, dragging her toward the gap.

She clawed at the stone, but her palms slid against the wet surface. The fissure widened, swallowing the faint glow, pulling her down.

And just as she lost her grip, something unseen caught her, hands that weren't hands, fingers made of shadow and pressure. They cradled her weight, guiding her not into the crack but deeper along a side tunnel she hadn't noticed before.

Her scream choked off in her throat as the darkness carried her, pulling her farther from the voices.

Jared. Emma.

She had been close. So close.

But now the caves had claimed her again.

25

The Cry in the Deep

THE TUNNEL BREATHED. That was the only word Jared could think of for the way the air moved around them, slow, rhythmic, as if the stone inhaled and exhaled in time with something sleeping far below. Their boots splashed through shallow water that shimmered with the lantern's last, wavering glow.

Then it came: a sound so faint that at first he thought it was the groan of shifting rock.

A voice.

"...help..."

Emma froze mid-step. "Did you hear that?"

Jared's heart clenched. The word was small, brittle, but real. "Lila."

It came again, warped by distance, but clearer this time. "Jared... please..."

The echo carried down a side passage veiled in mist. The sound of it hit them all differently. Emma's eyes filled instantly, lips trembling. Jared felt adrenaline burn away exhaustion, his whole body ready to sprint. But Marcus, Marcus went still. His head tilted slightly, listening with that eerie calm he'd worn since his return.

"That isn't her," he said softly. "Not anymore."

Emma spun on him, fury breaking through the fear. "Don't you dare say that!"

Marcus didn't meet her eyes. "You don't understand. It's calling through her. The same thing that kept me alive."

Jared shoved past him. "Then it's using her voice to tell us where she is. I'm not leaving her down here."

The air shifted again, cold sweeping past their legs like water receding from shore. The faint voice came once more, this time higher, desperate, real.

"Emma... I can see you... please..."

Emma bolted before Jared could stop her. The tunnel twisted, sloping downward, the mist thickening into a clinging fog. The lantern light flickered as Jared chased her, Marcus following silently behind.

They burst into a wide cavern, the ceiling lost above the fog. Water dripped from unseen heights into dark pools. The echoes made it impossible to tell where the voice came from.

"Lila!" Emma's shout broke apart in the mist. "Where are you?"

The fog shifted, slowly, deliberately. A silhouette formed within it, fragile and human. Lila.

Emma took a step forward. "She's there!"

But Jared grabbed her arm. "Wait."

The shape didn't move like it should. Its head lolled slightly to one side, its outline blurring as if the fog clung to it like skin. The faint glow of the lantern made its features shimmer, too smooth, too still.

Then the figure whispered: "You're so close."

The sound wasn't echoed. It was inside their heads. Emma yanked free and stumbled toward the shadow, tears streaming. Jared lunged after her. "Emma, stop!"

The ground shuddered. The mist parted, and the figure vanished. In its place, the floor cracked open, forming a narrow pit that breathed warm, foul air. Emma dropped to her knees at its edge, staring into it.

"Lila?"

From the depths came the faintest reply: "Down here..."

Jared grabbed Emma's shoulders, dragging her back. "It's trying to pull you in."

Marcus's voice came from behind them, calm and distant. "She's still alive. Just not where you think."

Jared spun, anger flaring. "Then where is she?!"

Marcus glanced toward the pit, eyes glinting with some quiet, dreadful knowledge. "Deeper. The shadows took her. They're not enemies. They serve what she was."

"What she was?" Jared repeated, voice rising.

But Marcus said nothing more. He only stared into the pit, the faint black veins along his neck pulsing in rhythm with the heartbeat of the cave.

Far below, unseen, something moved, and somewhere within that endless dark, Lila remembered a name.

Not Jared. Not Emma. Her own, but twisted, ancient, worn down by centuries of silence.

The Echoed One

She didn't know what it meant. But the shadows that carried her whispered softly, lovingly, like servants addressing their queen.

"Soon, you'll remember everything."

26

What the Shadows Told Him

THE PIT EXHALED a low, rhythmic breath that made the lantern flicker. Jared stood at its edge, fists clenched, staring into the black where Lila's voice had vanished. Emma knelt nearby, tears streaking the dirt on her cheeks, whispering her sister's name like a prayer.

Marcus stood apart. The shadows around him seemed thicker, as if they clung to him the way damp air clung to stone.

Jared turned, anger finally breaking through the fear. "You knew."

Marcus didn't look at him. "I suspected."

"You knew!" Jared's voice cracked through the cavern like a whip. "You said they took her. You said they serve her. How the hell would you know that unless—"

"Because they spoke to me."

The words froze Jared mid-step. Even Emma lifted her head, eyes wide.

Marcus finally turned to face them. His face was pale, streaked with grime, but his eyes... his eyes were calm in a way that didn't fit this place. "After it dragged me away. After you thought I was dead. I didn't die. I fell."

He gestured toward the pit, toward the endless dark below. "There's a whole world beneath this. Caverns that breathe. Walls that remember. I landed in one of them, alive, somehow. And then the dark came. It touched me. Not to kill me, not to feed, but to... speak."

Jared's stomach turned. "You're saying you talked to it?"

Marcus nodded slowly. "Not in words. In impressions. Images. They poured into me, centuries of memory, of what this place was before it drowned in shadow."

Emma rose shakily to her feet, clutching her arms around herself. "What did they show you?"

Marcus's voice dropped to a whisper. "Her. Lila. Before all of this. Before the village was swallowed. The shadows called her their light."

Emma flinched as if struck. "No. No, she's not, she's my sister. She's—"

Marcus took a hesitant step closer, but Jared moved between them, the lantern shaking in his hand. "Stay back."

"I'm not your enemy, Jared."

"Then start acting like it."

Marcus's jaw tightened. "You think I wanted this? You think I asked for their voices? I can't stop hearing them. Even now they're whispering, telling me which tunnels breathe, which ones kill. That's why we're alive."

Jared's throat went dry. "You sound like them."

Marcus's expression softened, almost pitying. "That's because I've seen what's coming. This place doesn't want death. It wants remembrance. It's using us to bring something back."

Emma's voice trembled. "Lila…"

"Yes," Marcus said quietly. "But not as she was. They called her The Echoed One. And they said she's waking up."

The silence that followed was heavy enough to break bone.

Jared's fingers tightened around the lantern's handle until his knuckles went white. "You expect us to believe that?"

"I expect nothing." Marcus's eyes flicked toward the pit again. "But if you want to see her again, we have to go down there. The shadows won't let her find her way back alone."

Emma took a shaky step toward the edge, staring into the dark that seemed to pulse with her sister's faint voice.

Jared grabbed her arm. "No. We don't even know what's real anymore."

She looked at him, her expression hollow. "Does it matter? If she's still down there, we can't leave her."

Marcus turned his face toward the tunnel leading down. His voice came out low, distant, almost reverent. "It's already begun. The air's changing. The walls are remembering her. She's calling them home."

The shadows along the rock trembled, almost in response.

Jared looked between them, the woman he couldn't protect and the man who might already belong to the dark, and felt something inside him crack.

They were still together. But for the first time, he realized they weren't a group anymore. Just three survivors walking at the edge of something vast, ancient, and patient enough to wait for them to destroy themselves.

27
What Was Forgotten

LILA DRIFTED IN THE DARK. Not falling. Not standing. Suspended, like the moment between waking and a nightmare where the mind pretends it's still safe.

The shadows held her gently, countless unseen hands moving with the rhythm of a heartbeat that wasn't hers. Their whispers wrapped around her skull, a lullaby sung in a language she almost recognized.

"Remember."

The word pulsed through her veins.

She saw flashes, faces that weren't Emma's, places that weren't the village. Stone halls bathed in pale light, a sky that burned silver instead of blue. She stood at the center of it all, crowned in smoke, her name echoing through the air. But it wasn't Lila.

It was older. Heavier. Ly'ahna.

The sound of it made the shadows tremble with reverence.

Her head ached. "Stop," she whispered, clutching her temples. "Please stop."

But the memories came anyway, rushing like a river through a broken dam.

She remembered why she came here. The thing that hunted her. The one that wanted to end her quest before it began. The ancient will that hated the light she carried. It followed her across lifetimes, feeding on every world that sheltered her until she found this one.

And so she had hidden herself, by cutting away everything she was. Every memory, every name. The ritual burned her soul down to its seed and buried it in flesh newly born.

She had become human. Lila.

A child adopted by a kind family in a quiet town.

Emma's family.

Her pulse quickened. Emma.

She saw her now, a small girl chasing sunlight through the trees, Lila's own laughter following close behind. Sisters. Not by blood, but by something deeper, the curse she had laid to bind them together.

It had been meant as protection. A veil. If her enemies came for her again, they would see only an ordinary life: two sisters, one unknowingly bearing the fragment of the other's soul.

But curses don't age gently.

Emma had grown, and with her the mark on her spirit. The streak of sickness that sometimes surfaced in fever dreams, the whispers that no priest could silence. It was the echo of Ly'ahna's power, leaking through the seal, poisoning and protecting all at once.

Now, as the shadows carried Lila deeper through the living caverns, she felt the curse tugging, like a string stretched tight between their hearts. The closer she drew to herself, the more Emma would suffer.

She wanted to cry out, to tell the shadows to stop, to let Emma live out her small, bright life untouched by this ancient horror. But the shadows only whispered back:

"You cannot stop the remembering. You made us for this."

Lila's breath hitched. Made them?

The darkness shifted around her, taking form, a thousand indistinct faces carved from smoke and memory. They bowed their heads.

"We were your wardens. Your hands in the dark. You told us to wait until you called again. And now you call."

The realization crashed over her like cold water. These were not servants of the enemy. These were hers. Born of her will, fragments of the void she had bent to her purpose.

But they were incomplete. Without her, they had wandered, feeding on the village above, twisting its people into offerings to keep her hidden. They had built a prison around her tomb and forgotten it was a sanctuary.

Lila pressed a hand to her chest. The shadows thrummed beneath her touch. "Emma," she whispered. "She's the last piece, isn't she? The part of me you couldn't reach."

The shadows pulsed once, agreement.

"She's the reason I'm still human."

Another pulse.

Lila closed her eyes. "Then she's also the reason I have to wake."

The cavern trembled softly. Far above, faint echoes of voices, Jared's anger, Emma's tears, Marcus's calm dread, filtered down through the stone. The sound of them filled her with warmth and sorrow in equal measure.

"Don't follow me," she whispered to the air, though she knew they couldn't hear. "You'll only remember too."

But the shadows stirred. "They are already remembering. Especially the marked one."

Lila froze. "Emma?"

The darkness rippled like laughter. "Her curse is breaking."

The revelation struck deeper than fear. The curse had been her safeguard. If it broke before she was whole again, Emma would die.

Lila felt the ancient fire inside her stir, the power she'd buried centuries ago, pushing through the fragile shell of her humanity. She gritted her teeth, forcing it down. "Not yet," she hissed. "Not until she's safe."

The shadows obeyed, swirling tighter around her.

And deep in the black, the thing she had fled, the one that hunted her light, shifted for the first time in an age. It could feel her awakening.

The chase would begin again.

28

The Weight of Souls

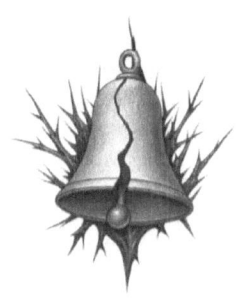

THE SHADOWS PARTED. Lila floated within a hollow chamber vast as a cathedral, its walls glimmering with faint, ghostly light. She realized with a shudder that it wasn't stone glowing around her. It was faces.

Hundreds. Thousands.

Each one half-formed, pressed into the black like insects in amber. Their mouths opened and closed soundlessly, but she heard them anyway: cries, prayers, the endless murmuring of the lost.

The souls of the village.

They had been here all along, trapped in the marrow of the earth. Their eyes rolled toward her as one, seeing her not as a stranger but as something long awaited.

The shadows whispered around her like a choir:

"They were promised release. You promised."

Lila's breath hitched. Memory bloomed behind her eyes, flashes of ritual circles, torches guttering in the wind, her own voice chanting words that bent the air around her.

"I was trying to save them," she whispered. "When the darkness came through the well, I sealed it here. I bound it, to myself. But it took them too. It took everyone."

The nearest faces stirred, mouths trembling as if begging her to continue.

The truth unfolded like a wound reopening. Long ago, when the veil between worlds had torn, the thing she now remembered as the Devourer had risen from the space beyond life, an intelligence made of hunger, a void that consumed memory itself. It sought to erase the concept of remembrance, to leave every world hollow and forgotten.

She had been chosen, not born, to stand against it.

Ly'ahna, the Keeper of Echoes…The Echoed one.

Her power was to remember. To hold the stories of the dead so they would not vanish. And when the Devourer reached this place, she had made her stand here, in this village built above the crossing point.

But she had failed.

The ritual that should have banished the Devourer's essence had shattered her own. To trap it, she had given up her immortality, embedding her consciousness into the mortal world, her soul scattered into new flesh and blood.

Emma's family had been the line she anchored herself to. Every generation carried a fragment of her essence. Emma was the last, and most potent, because the seal was failing. The curse that kept the Devourer bound was breaking, and Emma's life was the thread holding it closed.

Lila reached toward the faces. "If I can finish what I began, I can free you."

The souls' eyes shimmered with hope and terror.

The shadows stirred, shifting like wind-blown ash.

"You cannot face it alone. The others, the ones who followed you, carry the keys."

"Jared... Emma... Marcus."

The names reverberated through the chamber, stirring faint echoes from the walls.

"The protector, the bloodline, and the broken bridge."

"The bridge?" Lila asked softly.

"The man who hears us," the shadows said, their voices overlapping into one. "He walks between the living and the bound. Through him, the Devourer whispers, and through him, you may reach it."

Marcus.

Of course. The darkness that had touched him had not infected him. It had chosen him. The shadows had made him an instrument of connection, a vessel linking her sealed world to theirs. Through Marcus, she could guide them.

But she also knew what that meant: the Devourer could reach through him as well. He was both door and key. If Jared turned against him fully, they'd be lost before the ritual could even begin.

The souls shifted restlessly, their murmuring growing louder. She felt their desperation pulling at her like the tide.

"Tell me what to do," she whispered.

"Return to the crossing."

The image came to her mind, clearer than memory: the old well at the village center. The wound in the world where everything had started. It was the lock. The Devourer was still coiled beneath it, feeding on what it trapped. She had to go back, open it, and face it one last time.

"But I can't open the seal without killing Emma," she said. "Her life is the anchor."

"That is why the protector must choose," the shadows murmured. "One life for many. Or one soul reborn to bear it all."

The prophecy. She had written it herself, centuries ago.

The Keeper would rise again when the seal thinned, aided by three:

The Protector, who would guard her mortal half.

The Bloodline, whose curse bound the seal.

The Bridge, who could walk the space between.

And when the moment came, one of them would have to surrender everything to end the cycle, either to restore her or to free the souls forever.

Lila's pulse quickened. "No. There has to be another way."

But the shadows only whispered:

"You've known the price since you made it."

The faces in the walls began to hum, light rippling through their hollow eyes.

Their voices blended into a single, fragile plea.

"Remember us."

Tears burned her eyes. She reached out, touching the nearest face. It was warm. Soft. The soul within shuddered, and the light inside it brightened.

She could feel them now, every life lost to her failure. Farmers, children, mothers, soldiers, centuries of voices bound in stone. She could hear their laughter, their fear, and their dying prayers.

"I will," she whispered. "I swear it. This time, I'll finish it."

The shadows rippled with satisfaction.

"Then wake, Keeper. The others are waiting."

Lila's hand began to glow where it touched the stone. Light spread outward like veins of molten gold, crawling across the chamber. The faces sighed, their expressions softening.

Far above, in the tunnels where Jared, Emma, and Marcus stood at the edge of the pit, the walls began to pulse faintly with the same golden light.

Emma gasped, clutching her chest as the mark of her curse flared bright beneath her skin.

Jared looked around, wild-eyed. "What's happening?"

Marcus closed his eyes, listening. His lips moved, whispering words he didn't understand but somehow remembered.

"She's waking up."

29
The Rising Light

THE WALLS BEGAN TO BREATHE again. That was how it felt, slow waves of motion beneath the stone, the faint pulse of something alive spreading through the tunnels. A golden glow seeped through cracks in the rock, dim at first, then growing stronger until the shadows no longer belonged to their lantern.

Emma fell to her knees, clutching her chest. The light beneath her skin blazed through her shirt, tracing the web of veins along her collarbone like molten glass. Her scream echoed off the walls, raw and animal.

Jared dropped beside her.

"Emma, Emma, look at me!"

She tried to speak but only a gasp escaped. Her pupils were wide, unfocused, like someone looking at two worlds at once.

"It's the curse," Jared said, panic flooding his voice. "It's burning her alive."

Marcus crouched opposite him, eyes fixed on the glow. "Not burning," he said softly. "Calling."

Jared's head snapped up. "What?"

Marcus didn't answer right away. His hand hovered over Emma's shoulder, hesitant, as though touching her might pull him into the same current. "She's linked to it, to her. The light you see isn't killing her. It's remembering her."

Emma convulsed, gasping through clenched teeth. "She's... inside me," she whispered. "I can hear her."

Jared's pulse hammered. "We have to get her out of here."

Marcus met his eyes, the glow reflecting in his darkened pupils. "You don't understand. There's nowhere to go. It's all part of her. The well, the tunnels, this—" He gestured around them, voice trembling for the first time since his return. "It's waking up because she's waking up."

The golden light surged again, flaring through the stone like veins of fire. For an instant Jared saw shapes inside it, faces, hands, the outlines of people pressed into the rock. They were moving, not trapped anymore but stirring.

"The souls," Marcus murmured. "She's freeing them."

Jared swallowed hard. "And you just happen to know that? How do we know this isn't another trick? Another one of the voices?"

Marcus's jaw tightened. "Because they're not whispering now. They're singing."

He placed his palm flat against the wall. The stone pulsed once, and for a moment Jared saw the veins of black that had crept up Marcus's arm glow faintly gold. The veins didn't look diseased now. They looked like they belonged.

"I can feel her," Marcus said quietly. "The same way she felt them. She's trying to reach us."

Emma groaned, her breathing slowing. The light around her dimmed slightly, though it still pulsed beneath her skin. "She's scared," she whispered. "She doesn't remember everything yet. But she's coming back."

Jared glanced at Marcus. The man looked exhausted, the shadows under his eyes deep as bruises, but the calm in his expression wasn't the eerie detachment from before. It was focus. Resolve.

"What happens when she does re-member?" Jared asked.

Marcus looked up, and for once his voice held something almost human, fear wrapped in wonder.

"Then she'll need us."

The glow in the tunnels dimmed, shrinking back into cracks and seams. The golden veins faded to faint embers, leaving them in darkness once more, but the silence that followed was different. Not empty. Waiting.

Emma's breathing steadied. Jared helped her sit, his hands shaking. She leaned against him, eyes closed.

Marcus stood and turned toward the downward path where the glow had first ap-peared. The walls there still glimmered faintly, forming a faint spiral pattern de-scending into the earth.

"The way back," he murmured.

Jared rose, lantern in hand, though it was hardly needed, the faint light seemed to move with them now, as if the cavern itself guided their steps. He studied Marcus for a long moment.

"Alright," he said finally. "You lead."

Marcus nodded once, and for the first time since his return, Jared didn't argue.

Together, they stepped into the golden dark.

30
The Bell and the Hunger

THE CLIMB TOWARD THE WELL felt endless. The air thickened with the scent of iron and rain, though no rain had fallen in centuries. The faint golden veins that had guided them now flickered erratically, pulsing faster, as if the earth itself were afraid.

Emma stumbled, clutching her chest again. The light under her skin flared and dimmed with each heartbeat.

"She's close," Marcus murmured. "Too close."

Jared steadied Emma and glanced upward. "Then we move faster."

But even as he said it, the tunnels began to change. The walls pulsed once, then went dark, their smooth surfaces turn-

ing slick and black again. A sound rose from every direction, a low moan that wasn't quite a voice, as though the mountain itself had begun to breathe through broken lungs.

Marcus froze mid-stride. His pupils constricted.

"It's waking."

"What is?" Jared demanded.

"The other one," Marcus whispered. "The thing she bound here. The Devourer."

The light from the lantern stuttered and died. For a moment, there was only darkness, thick, wet, absolute. Then, from deep within it, a note rang out: a single, mournful tone that vibrated through their bones.

The bell.

It didn't come from his bell - or did it? Jared felt for it, his hand brushed the cold metal shape still tucked against his belt, but this wasn't that bell. This sound was older, vast. It rolled through the rock like thunder trapped in a grave.

Emma gasped. "It's the same sound from the tower."

Marcus nodded slowly, eyes distant. "That small bell was imbued with a portion of her power. When she failed the last time, she took a fragment of her power and cast it into the metal of the bell to bind the Devourer. Every toll is her voice, her command to hold the dark at bay. That bell was a treasured possession of someone from her lineage that was consumed and used by the darkness. However, what you are hearing is echoing from Lila herself."

Marcus took a slow steady breath, "…and the other one you hear from the distance is an insidious sound used by the Devourer. It is an overlay of all the souls is has taken over the centuries, all screaming out at once."

Jared's pulse hammered. "Then why is it ringing now?"

"Because the Devourer is waking, and trying to drown out Lilia's will."

The sound deepened, now two tones, colliding, scraping, one pure and golden, the other low and guttural. The clash made the air quiver. The walls began to bleed darkness; tendrils seeped from the cracks, curling toward them.

Marcus stumbled, clutching his head. "It's in me," he gasped. "It's pushing through the bridge."

Jared grabbed his shoulders. "Fight it!"

Marcus's teeth gritted. "I'm trying, she's trying—" His voice fractured. Then, in a burst of effort, he tore the smaller bell from Jared's belt and slammed it against the wall.

The tone that erupted wasn't metal. It was light. A blinding column of sound that carved through the tunnel, scattering the tendrils like smoke in wind. The golden resonance hummed, pure and steady, and Jared realized the pure song-like tone from before and the one from the small bell he carried were the same song, separated only by distance and time.

When the light faded, Marcus sagged against the stone, trembling. His voice was barely audible.

"She made it to answer the Devourer. The bell's a piece of her soul. That's why it helps us, it's trying to find its source again."

Jared grabbed the bell and put it back around his belt.

Emma knelt beside him. The glow under her skin pulsed in rhythm with the bell's fading echo. "And when it finds her?"

Marcus lifted his head, eyes wet with pain and awe.

"Then she'll be whole."

The tunnels shook once, hard enough to drop them to their knees. A gust of wind blasted upward from the depths, hot, stinking of rot. The Devourer was moving now, its presence a tidal wave pressing up from beneath.

Jared hauled Marcus to his feet. "Then we need to reach her before it does."

They pushed on; the stone slick underfoot, the bell's tone fading to a heartbeat's thrum. The tunnel narrowed into a spiral passage. And then, suddenly, it opened.

They stood at the mouth of the well.

What had once been stone was now alive with light. The entire shaft glowed from within; threads of gold racing upward like veins of molten dawn. The wind poured out in steady waves, carrying with it the sound of whispers, no longer mournful, but singing.

At the bottom, half-buried in radiant mist, stood Lila.

She hovered inches above the ground, eyes closed, and her hair lifting as though underwater. The shadows around her bent, not menacing but reverent, orbiting her like planets around a star. Every beat of her heart sent ripples of light crawling up the walls.

Jared stopped breathing. "Lila…"

Emma's tears shone in the golden glow. "She's remembering."

Marcus sank to one knee, head bowed. "She's awakening."

The bell at Jared's belt began to hum softly, resonating with her light. Lila's eyes opened, two blazing suns of gold and shadow, and for the first time since the village had died, the darkness trembled in fear.

31
The Last Light Before the Storm

FOR A HEARTBEAT the world held its breath.

The glow from the well dimmed and steadied, settling into a soft radiance that painted everything in gold. Jared felt warmth spread through the stone under his palms, real warmth, not the fevered heat of the Devourer's taint. Emma's hand found his. They stood together, staring down into the pit where Lila waited.

She was no longer just the woman he'd known. The lines of her face were the same, yet otherworldly; her skin shimmered faintly, veins of light pulsing beneath it like living script. When she looked up, her eyes caught theirs, and for a moment Jared swore the years between them vanished, no pain, no hunger, no dark.

"Lila…" Emma's voice cracked. She started forward, but Jared's arm caught her gently.

Lila smiled, faint, human, fragile. "You came back."

Her voice echoed strangely, doubled, one tone her own and the other something older, deeper. It made the air hum. Marcus descended the final steps, the golden glow haloing him; when he reached the bottom, the light around her seemed to brighten, as though recognizing its missing piece.

"You did this," Lila said softly to him. "You carried the bridge."

Marcus bowed his head. "I only followed the sound."

Jared descended next, the cracked bell clinking faintly against his belt. Lila's gaze dropped to it, her expression softening. "The soul bearer… you kept it."

"It nearly killed us," Jared said, though the bitterness had gone out of his voice.

"It nearly killed me first." Her hand lifted, trembling slightly, and the cracked metal resonated in answer, a faint, clear hum that threaded through the air. "When it rings, the Devourer stirs. When it breaks, the seal fails completely."

Marcus's eyes widened. "It's cracked."

"I know." Her smile faltered. "That means we're running out of time."

The cavern shuddered, a low tremor that rippled up from the depths. Dust fell from the walls in soft gray curtains. Lila turned her gaze toward the pit below her feet, where the golden mist had begun to darken.

"I need to finish what I began," she said. "The souls are bound to this place, held between remembrance and oblivion. The Devourer feeds on their silence. I must open the seal and free them before it consumes everything."

Emma stepped closer, her light answering Lila's in tiny pulses. "And my curse?"

Lila's face softened with sorrow. "You were never cursed, Emma. You were the part of me that remembered how to love. The bond between us is what hid me from the Devourer. But if I break the seal, that bond must end. The light in you will return to me."

Emma shook her head, tears slipping free. "If that happens—"

"I'll take it gently," Lila said. "I promise."

Another tremor. The golden light in the well twisted abruptly, swirling downward as if sucked through a drain. A sound rose from the dark, wet, dragging, immense.

The Devourer was waking.

The air filled with the smell of cold earth and rot. The walls bled black, the light retreating as tendrils of shadow slithered upward. The singing of the souls turned to screams.

Marcus staggered, clutching his head. "It's pushing through me, trying to use the bridge!"

Lila's eyes flared bright. "Hold fast, Marcus. You are not its vessel. You are mine."

She reached toward him. Light shot from her fingertips, weaving through the air and wrapping around him like bands of gold. His body arched, the black veins beneath his skin glowing, burning away into light.

The Devourer screamed, a sound that tore through the stone and into their bones. From the pit below, a shape began to rise: vast, amorphous, its surface rippling like liquid shadow. Eyes bloomed and vanished across it, thousands of them, each reflecting Lila's light as though mocking her.

Emma pressed against Jared, trembling. "What is that—"

"The end of memory," Lila whispered. "The void that eats all stories. It's come to stop me before I can finish the telling."

She turned to Jared, gaze fierce now. "You still carry the bell. When I call, you must ring it once more with all your might. The crack will split the soul bearer completely and let the light through. That will free the souls, and me. But you must not hesitate."

The creature's mass hit the chamber floor, sending shockwaves through the rock. Lila lifted her hands, light roaring from her body like a sun breaking through storm clouds.

"Go!" she shouted. "Back to the rim, ring it when I tell you!"

Jared grabbed Emma's arm, dragging her toward the stairs. The bell at his waist vibrated violently, pulling against its strap as if it longed to leap into the light.

Behind them, Lila rose higher, her voice carrying through the cavern like the echo of a thousand lives remembering their names.

32
The Bell at the Edge of Memory

THE AIR SHOOK with the sound of two worlds colliding. Lila's light had become a storm, blades of gold cutting through the darkness as the Devourer rose from the pit like a sea of shadow given form. Its scream was not heard so much as felt, vibrating through bone, through memory, through the stories of everyone who had ever lived in this valley.

Jared and Emma reached the ledge above, the broken bell at his waist pulsing like a heartbeat. Every toll of it sent pain through his ribs; every beat felt like a question he wasn't ready to answer.

He looked down. Lila was radiant and terrible, a figure of living sunlight, her arms spread wide as the shadows tried to swallow her whole. Each strike of the Devourer's tendrils left gouges in the light, but she pushed back, every movement answering with a flare that burned holes in the dark. It was a war between silence and remembrance.

Marcus stood halfway down the slope, one hand pressed to his chest, the golden bands around him still glowing faintly. He was whispering again, his voice carrying the rhythm of Lila's pulse. Whatever she was doing, she needed him alive to anchor it.

Jared's hands clenched around the bell. The crack across its surface gleamed, thin and bright, like a wound that refused to heal. Lila's last words echoed inside him:

"When I call, ring it. Don't hesitate."

But his mind screamed questions she hadn't answered.

Would ringing it destroy her? Would it kill Emma? Or him? Could one act both save and erase everything he'd fought to protect?

He'd lost so much already, the world above, the people turned to stone, Marcus for a time, and nearly Emma too. Now the sound of that single bell would decide if any of it had meaning.

Below, the Devourer surged. Its shadow stretched toward Lila, swallowing the floor, swallowing the walls, swallowing the light itself. Her voice rose, not a scream, but a song. The melody threaded through the darkness, pure and defiant, the same tone Jared had heard in the bell's faint hum.

"Emma!" Lila's voice carried upward, layered with a thousand echoes. "Your light is mine, but your heart is yours. Let me bear the weight so you can remember what I forgot."

Emma dropped to her knees, her skin blazing with gold. The air around her shimmered. Her mouth opened, but the words that came out were not hers:

"Take it back, sister."

The light ripped free. It left her body in a violent burst, tearing through the air as a column of brilliance that struck Lila squarely in the chest. The impact rocked the cavern. For an instant Lila's form flickered, half human, half divine.

She screamed, but not in pain, in release.

The Devourer roared back, its surface splitting, thousands of eyes opening to pour darkness over her. It struck.

Lila raised her hands. The shadows hit her like a tidal wave, blotting out the light. The entire cavern went black.

"JARED!" Marcus's voice cut through the dark, desperate, but not his. "NOW!" This was the sound of Lilia's voice. It was flowing through Marcus as if it was his own.

Jared's heart stopped. His fingers trembled over the bell. He wanted to run, to hide, to do anything but face what came next. But then he saw them, faces appearing all around him in the stone, faint outlines glowing through the black: the souls waiting, watching. Not pleading this time. Trusting.

He swallowed the fear. "For all of you," he whispered. "And for her."

He raised the bell high and struck it once, hard.

The crack split wide. The sound that burst forth was not a ring but a release: light pouring as sound, sound pouring as memory. It flooded the cavern, rushing downward in waves. Every face in the stone turned bright, every trapped soul crying out in joy.

The Devourer shrieked, its body unraveling, black strands burning away like smoke in a gale. Lila stood at the center of it, her silhouette burning brighter and brighter until it hurt to look at her.

"Remember me," she whispered. Her voice reached Emma's mind like a touch. "Not as a god. As your sister."

And then the light consumed everything.

33
The Last Echo

SILENCE. It came after the light, slowly, like the tide withdrawing from a broken shore. The roar of collapsing stone faded, and what remained was stillness.

The kind that lives after endings.

Jared blinked through the dust. The cavern had changed. The black walls that once pulsed with shadow now gleamed pale gold, their surfaces smooth and warm beneath his trembling hands. The air smelled of rain after drought, clean, impossible.

Emma knelt nearby, light still faintly pulsing under her skin, though weaker now, almost human again. Her eyes shone with tears, but not from pain. She was whispering something, soft, reverent.

Lila's name.

Marcus stood farther off, leaning against a fragment of broken pillar, his face streaked with soot. The glow that had traced his veins had vanished. For the first time in what felt like forever, he looked mortal.

Jared followed Emma's gaze. At the heart of the cavern, where the Devourer's pit had been, there was only light, a swirling column of gold and white, rising like breath. In its center, a figure drifted.

Lila.

Her form flickered, more spirit than flesh, each heartbeat fading into brilliance. The Devourer was gone; its scream had ended in silence, its vast shadow dissolved into the same light that now held her. She had done it.

The prophecy had come full circle.

Lila's eyes opened one last time. They found Emma first.

"It's done."

The voice was gentle, no longer split between human and divine. Just hers.

Emma stumbled forward, falling to her knees. "Don't go. Please, not again."

Lila smiled, a soft, weary smile that carried the peace of lifetimes.

"You were never meant to carry my curse forever. You were my memory, Emma. The part of me that loved enough to stay human. I'm giving that back to you now."

A soft wind brushed through the chamber. Emma gasped as the last trace of light left her chest, flowing toward Lila like a shimmering thread. When it touched her, Lila shuddered, and her edges grew brighter, too bright.

"Lila!" Jared shouted. He took a step closer but stopped, the heat of the light forcing him back. "You don't have to—"

"I do," she said, her voice like a fading song. "The seal is whole again. The Devourer's name has been forgotten. As long as I remember it, it cannot return. That is my final task."

Her gaze turned to Marcus. "You kept the bridge open when I could not reach. For that, I give you peace."

Marcus's breath hitched. The faint hum that had haunted him since the shadows touched his mind finally stilled. He closed his eyes, tears cutting clean paths through the grime. "Then I'll remember you for both of us."

Lila smiled again, the gold around her deepening into a warm amber glow. "You will forget in time. All of you will. That's the mercy of it."

She looked last at Emma, her expression soft but certain. "Live a long life, sister. Tell stories. Fill the silence I leave behind."

The light surged once more, rising until the cavern blazed like dawn. Her outline dissolved into it, spreading out in a spiral that wound upward through the tunnel toward the world above. It carried with it a soft, final sound, one pure note, like the ring of a bell made whole.

Then she was gone.

The well was no longer a wound. Just a quiet pool of light, fading slowly as if the earth were healing.

Jared fell to his knees, bowing his head. Emma stood in silence, her hand pressed to her heart. The mark there had vanished, leaving only warmth. She exhaled slowly, the first breath she'd taken in peace since the curse began.

Marcus looked toward the tunnel leading upward. "She did it," he said. "It's over."

Jared nodded, voice raw. "The prophecy's fulfilled."

Above them, faint and distant, the first hint of morning filtered through the cracks, real sunlight, reaching places it hadn't touched in an age. The world had changed. Quietly. Completely.

Emma whispered into the new light, a small smile trembling on her lips.

"Goodbye, Lila."

And in that breath of dawn, for just an instant, she thought she heard an answer, soft as a sigh, bright as memory:

"Remember."

34

The Sound That Remains

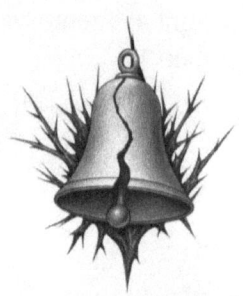

THEY LEFT THE WELL AT DAWN.
The light that poured from its depths had
softened into a quiet glow, no longer divine,
no longer dangerous. It shimmered gently
beneath the surface like sunlight on still water. Flowers had begun to grow around its
edge, pale white blooms that only opened in
morning light. It stood as it was meant to: a
place of remembrance, not ruin.

Jared lingered at the rim, the cracked
bell heavy at his belt. Emma stood beside
him, staring into the golden reflection below.

"She's really gone," she whispered.

Jared nodded. "No. She's home now."

Emma brushed at her eyes. "And the bell?"

He looked down at it, the crack that split it wide, the dull gleam where her light had once burned through it. "It doesn't ring anymore," he said softly. "Maybe it never will again."

Emma smiled faintly through her grief. "Maybe that's the point."

They stayed a little while longer, until the mist began to lift. Then they turned toward the valley path, leaving the well behind, its quiet glow watching them go.

Years passed. The world healed. Emma married, moved north, raised children who grew up hearing the story of a sister who had "traveled far away." Sometimes she dreamed of golden light flooding through cracks in the walls, or of a hand reaching from water to brush her cheek. She never told anyone about those dreams; they were hers alone.

Marcus became something of a legend himself; a wanderer who found forgotten shrines, sealed old wells, and spoke prayers in languages no one remembered teaching him. Those who met him said he carried peace with him, though his eyes always seemed to be listening to something far away.

And Jared stayed. He rebuilt the village as best he could, stone by stone. People came back over time, farmers, craftsmen, children laughing in the square where the bell tower once stood. Life resumed, ordinary and precious.

He never forgot the others. On quiet nights he would sit in his workshop, the small bell resting on a shelf beside his lantern. The crack along its rim ran deep, nearly splitting it in two. It caught the light like an old scar. He never tried to polish it. Some things, he decided, deserved to look the way they survived.

Sometimes, when he closed his eyes, he still heard her voice, the echo of Lila's last words to Emma:

"Tell stories. Fill the silence I leave behind."

And so he did. He told them to travelers, to children, to anyone who would listen, about a sister of light, a world of shadows, and a bell that once sang a god's name. Over decades, the tale became myth. Then it became only a whisper. Then it was nearly forgotten.

It was spring again, many years later. The house was quiet, dust swirling in sunlight. Jared's hair had turned white, his hands lined and strong. He had outlived the fear, outlived the memory of the tunnels. He moved to the shelf, fingers brushing the cracked bell.

It had not rung in half a lifetime.

He smiled to himself. "You earned your rest."

He turned away, light dimming through the window. Behind him, in the stillness, the faintest sound trembled through the air, a single, delicate chime.

He froze. Slowly, he looked back. The bell stood exactly where it always had. But the crack that split it wide was narrower now, a thin hairline instead of a wound. He leaned closer, heart pounding.

Another chime. Soft. Clear. Like a heartbeat.

For an instant the room glowed gold. Then it was gone.

Outside, the wind moved through the valley, carrying a whisper that might have been memory or might have been her voice.

"Remember."

And somewhere beyond sight, deep in the quiet places of the world, the faint echo of the bell continued to ring.

The End.